SHADRACH

SHADRACH

by Meindert DeJong
Pictures by Maurice Sendak

A HARPER TROPHY BOOK

HARPER & ROW, PUBLISHERS

NEW YORK

Cambridge
Hagerstown
Philadelphia
San Francisco

1817

London
Mexico City
São Paulo
Sydney

Library of Congress Catalog Card Number: 53–5250
ISBN 0-06-440115-4

First published in 1953. 12th printing, 1977.
First Harper Trophy edition, 1980.

For my big brother, Rem

SHADRACH

CHAPTER 1

There was this boy, Davie, and he was going to have a rabbit. His grandfather had promised it. A real, live rabbit! A little black rabbit, if possible. In a week, if possible. And this was in the Netherlands.

There was this boy, Davie, and he was going to have a rabbit in a week. And here he was, in his grandfather's barn on the first long afternoon of that long waiting week. He was lying in front of the empty rabbit hutch. He was peering into the hutch. He had a whole long week to wait for his rabbit, but he already had the hutch. His father had made it for him.

It was dark and quiet in the barn—so dark

1

that if he peered hard into the empty hutch, Davie could easily imagine a little black rabbit behind the narrow up-and-down slats that ran along the whole front of the hutch. In front of the row of up-and-down slats Davie's father had fixed a little slanting crib. That was to put clover and grass and dandelions and lettuce in. Then the little rabbit would push his wriggly black nose through the narrow spaces between the up-and-down slats and nibble the grass and clover and dandelions and lettuce. The grass, the clover, the dandelions and lettuce were already in the crib—even though the little rabbit was not coming for a week. Inside the hutch was a thick bed of gleaming yellow straw. And all the hutch lacked was a little black rabbit.

But he would be there in a week!

And what is a week? Poof—and like that a week is gone by. Poof—there is a good week, and poof—there it is gone. But a week doesn't go by, and doesn't go by, when you are waiting for a little black rabbit. Oh, a waiting week is long. It is like eternity.

"And that is long!" the boy said aloud in the dark barn to the little black rabbit that wasn't there.

Six long waiting days still to wait. And nothing left to do! The hutch was ready, the straw was ready, the food was ready in the crib. "Ah, little black rabbit," the boy said to the little rabbit that wasn't there.

Then he thought of it. He hadn't named the rabbit! You couldn't just go around saying: "Ah, little black rabbit."

It had to be a name that sounded black!

"Satan," he said aloud in the dark, quiet barn. No! What a name for a little rabbit with a wriggly little nose!

"Shoe Polish," he said aloud. Oh, man, no! What a sticky name.

"Night," he said, and listened to it. NO! No good.

Out of nowhere "Lily of the Valley" jumped into his mind. It sang itself inside of him—it became a song: "Lily of the Valley, fairest of ten thousand."

That was the way it had sung itself into his mind, and that was the way it made itself into a little song inside of him. It was from a hymn. But it was all wrong from the hymn. The hymn went "He's the Lily of the Valley, the bright and morning star. He's the fairest of ten thousand to my soul." It didn't go "Lily of the Valley, fairest of ten thousand." But that was the way his inside song was singing inside of him. He thought about it hard. The little black rabbit would be the fairest of ten thousand to his soul. But you couldn't call a little black rabbit "Lily of the Valley." Lilies were white. And you certainly couldn't call him "Fairest of Ten Thousand." When he had decided that, the little inside song shut itself off, and he sat still.

All of a sudden he knew. *Shadrach* was the rabbit's name. It even sounded black! He tried it on his tongue. He listened to it. *Shadrach*.

That was it! That was the rabbit's name!

"Shadrach," he said aloud. "Fairest of ten thousand," he said aloud. He sat yearning for his little black rabbit.

But Shadrach was a name from the Bible. And now he wasn't sure that it was right to name a rabbit with a name from the Bible. Shadrach was one of the three young men that old Nebuchadnezzar in the old testament had tossed into the fiery furnace—Shadrach, Meshach, and Abed-nego. Suddenly he thought that Shadrach must be a good black name—Shadrach must have got pretty black in that fiery furnace. He didn't smile, because it wasn't right to joke about things from the Bible, and he still didn't know whether you should name a rabbit with a name from the Bible. It worried him.

4

But he hadn't really named his little rabbit after the name in the Bible! Suddenly he thought of it. No! He was really calling the rabbit Shadrach after the to-bed-going game that his father had made up. It was an exciting game. His father would say "Shadrach," and toss him high without letting him go. His father would say "Meshach," and toss him still higher without letting him go. But then his father would say "And-Abed-We-Go," and let him fly into the high closet bed. He'd bounce up on the mattress and fall, bounce again and fall! Oh, it was a fine game, but now they never played it any more. Not after he'd been sick so long. It was too rough.

Now he knew! The name Shadrach had popped into his mind from the "And-Abed-We-Go" game that his father had made up for him —and not from the Bible. It had come to him because of the rabbit hutch that his father had made for him. That was why! He sat there loving his father for the hutch he had made for the little black rabbit. He sat longing for the little black rabbit. Shadrach was his name!

Now everything that could be done, had been done. The little rabbit even had a name. Now there was nothing more to do. But he had to do something! Even his skin prickled in his sudden restlessness. He poked with a finger at the greens in the crib. He decided they were wilted. Maybe he'd better get some new fresh greens for Shadrach. That's what he'd do! Everyday he'd fill the crib with new dandelions and clover and grass. Even though Shadrach wasn't there! It would almost make it feel as if Shadrach was there. It was a nice plan, it made him feel nice. Inside of him the little song started up again: "Shadrach. Shadrach. Fairest of ten thousand to my soul."

He looked around the barn for something in which he could put the greens he was going to gather. His eyes fell on a neat stack of folded burlap bags that Grandfather had piled right beside Shadrach's hutch. A great plan hit him. He wouldn't just go and get a handful of dandelions and clover. He knew where there was a big patch of clover. He'd gather a whole bagful, a whole bag full for Shadrach!

He tingled with the plan. He grabbed a sack and hurried to the door, and he carefully eased the big barn door open. The yard was bright with sunlight. He stood blinking. But when his eyes got used to the light he could see Grandma

6

across the yard still sleeping in the reed chair at the window. He smiled at his sleeping grandmother.

There she was still sleeping, and she'd already been asleep when he had sneaked out of

the high closet bed and out of the room and to the barn. He'd landed on the floor with quite a thump, too. But Grandma's head had just gone on nodding.

There she sat nodding over her knitting. Grandma always pretended she was knitting, but the moment she picked up her knitting she fell asleep. He smiled fondly, pleased that she still was sleeping, for now he could go out to get the bagful of clover. Why, Grandma was doing his sleeping for him! Mother took him to Grandmother's house every afternoon since he'd been so sick, because she thought he could sleep better there than in their own noisy house. He was supposed to be sleeping in the bed right now, but Grandmother was doing the sleeping for him in the reed chair. It was Grandma that did the sleeping.

Laughing at the thought, he edged out of the doorway for a quick dash across the yard and out of sight of Grandma's window. He knew a place where the clover was really thick and tall. It wouldn't take long with so much clover. He'd be back long before Grandma woke up. He looked at his sack. Oh, he'd forgotten about string. If he was going to stuff the bag really round full, it would have to be tied, otherwise the clover would come pushing right out. He dashed back into the barn to hunt for string.

He was busily hunting. The barn door slid open. Sunlight fell across his feet. He jumped. There stood his grandmother!

"Yes, I should think you would jump," Grandmother said. "Davie, Davie. You were hardly in bed at all, the bed was hardly rumpled. You sneaked out the moment I fell asleep."

He nodded. He nodded his head very fast, hoping and hoping that his grandmother wouldn't notice the sack squeezed under his

arm. "I couldn't sleep, so I just had to go and see the rabbit hutch that Dad made for me," he explained.

"As if you hadn't already seen it ten thousand times! You'll wear it out just from looking, Davie."

He chuckled. That was funny! Wearing a

rabbit hutch out from looking! It wasn't really so funny, but he chuckled and chuckled and meanwhile secretly let the sack slide to the ground.

Now Grandma was saying: "Well, you'll just have to go back to bed until supper time." She said it in such a special firm way, he knew it was no use to argue. Suddenly he didn't mind. He couldn't go after the clover now anyway, with Grandma awake, and there was nothing else to do in the whole long waiting afternoon. But in bed he could think about Shadrach, and about his new name, and about his coming, and everything about Shadrach. He wouldn't sleep, he'd just remember everything about Shadrach.

"The idea!" Grandma was saying. "Here your poor mother thinks you're sleeping and resting because she so badly wants you to get healthy and strong again, and you sit by the hour in a musty, dirty, damp barn!"

"But I am strong and healthy," he wanted to say. He didn't. He just let himself be led away, not saying anything of what he thought. Grandma was that way, and Mother was that way. It was no use talking. When he told them he wasn't sick any more, they just looked at him in a funny, unbelieving way. He was a school-

boy. He wasn't a baby who had to sleep afternoons. Just because you'd been sick, you didn't
stay sick! It was no use. Mother and Grandmother just seemed to want to keep him baby
sick, and make him sleep afternoons!

"The idea!" Grandmother sputtered while
she pulled his clothes off. "Hours in that barn,
and all for a rabbit that isn't even there. Your
grandfather should have known better than to
promise you that rabbit a week ahead of time."

He didn't listen. He climbed up the little lad-
der into the high bed. He'd go to bed, if he had
to, but he wouldn't sleep. He'd just lie there
and think and think everything about Shadrach.
"Shadrach. Little black rabbit. Fairest, fairest
of ten thousand." The inside happy song was
singing itself. He wouldn't sleep!

CHAPTER 2

It was nice lying there in bed with Grandma busy at the stove. Grandmother was bustling about getting supper ready against the time that Grandfather would come home from his little truck garden farm two miles outside the village. Now she was slicing thin white cold potatoes into the frying pan, and the frying pan was beginning to whisper little sounds. Now Grandma was putting the coffee in the pot. Grandmother made heavy noises as she walked about on the creaking floor. He, Davie, lay on his back with his eyes wide open, but he didn't turn his eyes toward Grandma. He was trying to guess what Grandmother was doing, just from the sounds.

Soon Grandpa would come home. And then this Monday afternoon would be sort of over. Then there'd be one day less to wait for Shadrach. And here only last Saturday—why, that was only two days ago, but it seemed an age— Grandpa had made the great sudden surprise promise of a little rabbit. In a week, if possible! Black, if possible! Davie wriggled himself down under the covers up to his mouth. Now he would think about it—how it had come—so sudden, so unexpected—the great promise of a rabbit. And it had all come about because he had helped Grandpa on Saturday to plant beans!

He had gone with Grandpa to the little truck garden farm way outside the village, for the air and sunshine. "It'll do him good," Grandpa had told Mother. "He's been sick. Now don't keep him baby sick. Air and sunshine is what he needs now. Look at him—pale as a toadstool on a compost pile!"

"The way you always put things," Mother had said to Grandpa. She hadn't smiled about that saying about the toadstools. And it was funny! But she had let him go with Grandpa.

Outside the village Grandpa had hoisted him to his shoulder and had carried him, although he was really a schoolboy now. He was glad Grandpa had waited to carry him until they were out of sight of the village, because he was

really a schoolboy. He just hadn't started school because he was just over being sick.

It had been a wonderful day—the out-in-the-country sky so high, the wind so clean, the sun soft and warm on his skin. Frogs had been singing in all the ditches. A skylark had been hanging in the sky straight above the little farm, singing his heart out.

"The frogs think they can do better. They're trying to outsing the lark," Grandpa had said. A big white stork had come sailing. The stork had gone stalking along the ditches on his stilts of legs, hunting frogs. That had stopped the frogs from trying to outsing the skylark all right—the frogs so quiet, the stork stalking white and tall, the lark still singing.

Grandpa had begun making little holes with his hoe—just so deep, just so round. Rows of little holes, marching across the land. It had seemed like some secret game Grandpa was playing.

"What are you making the holes for, Grandpa?"

"For beans. Beans and more beans. Lima beans!"

"Oh."

"Would you like to plant some, Davie?"

"Oh, I would!"

Grandfather had shown him. "Three white beans to a hole. No more, no less. Eyes down! Press them into the soil with their eyes down. One bean to each side of the hole, one to the front. So. . . ." Grandpa had said. "One ahead of the other two. He's the boss bean, he's the captain. So. . . . Beans, beans, marching across the land. Three beans to a hole, the captain bean ahead."

"Eyes down, Grandpa?" It hadn't seemed right. It had seemed upside down.

"Eyes down, Davie. Oh, yes, eyes down! That way they come up much faster. That way they can push their little humped backs right up through the soil. Yes, eyes down."

That way it had at once been a game. Grandpa had made it a game for him. Boss bean, captain bean, marching across the land. But they hadn't looked like soldiers. They had looked much more like little white pigs, rooting in the soil at the bottoms of the little cups of holes. Their snouts down, their little round backs showing white and humped. When he had finished the first row he had run all the way back just to see all the little white pigs marching across the land.

"Eyes down. Snouts down. And up they come,

up they come. Push their backs up through the soil, and up they come. Up they come."

That was how his little inside song had just suddenly started, because he was having such fun stooping along the row of empty holes with his bag of big white beans, setting the beans and singing his song. "And up they come. Up they come."

The inside song had no tune, not a tune like a hymn in church. It just had a work tune that made the work of planting the beans busy and important, that made it swing.

Grandpa had gone on making more holes.

"And up they come. Up they come. Eyes down, snouts down. Push their backs up through the soil, and up they come!"

Grandpa had suddenly crossed over from his row of holes to inspect the beans he had planted. Grandpa had been amazed! They were all planted just so, just the way Grandpa had told him to do it. Two beside each other, the captain bean ahead—only they were little pigs. Grandpa had been proud of him!

"How old are you?" Grandpa had asked. As if he didn't know! "Well, Davie, all I can say—I couldn't have done it better myself. It's perfect, just perfect."

That had made him feel good. So warm and good inside that his little song couldn't stay inside. It had sung out of him, even though Grandpa stood right there. And he had worked still harder.

Then Grandpa, finished with making holes, had crossed over to the first row, and had started filling the holes. It had seemed almost a shame to bury all the little white pigs of beans. But that was the way it had to be, because if they weren't buried, how could they come up? "And up they come. Up they come."

His song had had to go faster then, because Grandpa wasn't ahead of him any more. Grandpa was coming on behind him now, filling the holes very fast. And because his song went faster, it went louder, and Grandpa had heard. But it wasn't until Grandpa had filled the last hole with the last three beans that he had said: "So you make little work songs when you work."

"Oh, play songs, too, Grandpa, when I play," he had told Grandpa. "But I don't make them, they make themselves, and then they sing themselves inside of me, but sometimes they come out. It's fun."

They had stood there straightening out their tired backs. Grandpa had looked all around.

"Good grief, nobody in any of the fields any more. It must be I'm late again. It must be way past supper time. Yooie, am I going to catch it from Grandma. But it was nice here this afternoon, you and I, wasn't it?"

"Oh, Grandpa, yes!" He'd really been sorry the beans were all planted.

"But me keeping you out this long your first day out of the house—I'll catch it from your mother, too. Here, Beanstalk Jack, you get up on my shoulder, and I'll make seven league strides for home. I'm going to catch it all around!"

But Mother was Grandfather's daughter! It had seemed queer that Mother would scold her father for keeping him out late. He had thought hard about that as he jogged along on Grandfather's shoulders. Suddenly Grandpa had tilted his head back and had looked up at him. Then Grandpa had said it! "Davie, how would you like a rabbit? A real, live rabbit! Maybe a black rabbit."

"Oh!"

Just like that Grandpa had said it. And to think that until that moment he'd never even thought about a rabbit. Why, he hadn't even known there were all-black rabbits!

He couldn't believe it.

"In a week," Grandpa had said. "In a week, if possible. Black, if possible. Just as soon as Maartens, the chinaware man, comes to our village with his chinaware wagon."

"But you said a real, live rabbit—not chinaware!"

"But, Davie, didn't you know? Maartens also sells live rabbits. Often he comes to the village, and way back, tucked away in a corner of his chinaware wagon, he's got a boxful of rabbits."

It had been hard to believe, even though Grandfather had said so. He had marveled over it, because he'd often stood at Maarten's wagon with Mother and the other village women crowded around it. But he'd been so small—that was before he'd been sick so long—he couldn't look into the high wagon. All he could see were the cups and plates and things his mother and the other women took down from the wagon and showed to each other. Why, he'd been so small and shy then, Mother had even had to hold him by the hand. And all the time there had been live rabbits up on the wagon! And he hadn't known!

"When, Grandpa? When will Maartens come again?"

"Oh, not until next Saturday, a week from today. But tonight a letter goes out to him. 'Maartens, be sure to bring a rabbit when you come to our village next time. A little black rabbit, if possible. For Davie. . . .'" Grandpa had read it off as if it already stood in a letter.

"Oh, Grandpa!"

That had been last Saturday, and now Saturday was already two days ago, but it was still a miracle and a wonder. But now it wasn't unbelievable any more. Now it could be believed, because there was the hutch and the little slant crib and the food in the crib. The letter had gone out to Maartens. Maybe Maartens in that far away town had it even now. It sang through Davie all of a sudden: "Shadrach. Shadrach. Little black rabbit. Fairest of ten thousand to my soul." It was so happy, it almost sang itself out loud. He remembered to throw a hasty glance at Grandma, but she hadn't heard at the noisy stove. It could hardly be believed, it was so wonderful. . . .

Grandma startled him. "Davie," she said suddenly, "that's not sleeping. Nobody, just nobody but a fish, can sleep with his eyes wide open."

He hastily closed his eyes, tight.

The potatoes suddenly sizzled louder, crackled and sputtered with hot sputterings in the frying pan. Grandma had to turn back to the stove. It hit him, all of a sudden, the great plan! Tomorrow he would do it! Gather a whole sack full of clover for Shadrach. "Shadrach, Meshach, and Abed-we-go!" Hey! That's what he would do. Not just one sackful. Three whole sackfuls! "Shadrach, Meshach, and Abed-we-go."

The whole plan formed in his head. Tomorrow afternoon he'd sneak out of bed again, the moment Grandma fell asleep. This time he wouldn't land with a thump—he knew how now. This time he wouldn't sit in the barn looking at the hutch. He'd go right out to the big patch of clover. He knew just exactly where it was—along the road on the way to the village of Nes, right below the dike. Why, there was so much clover there, he'd be back long before Grandma woke up. There he'd be lying back in bed when Grandmother woke up, but all the time there'd be three big bags of clover in the barn right in front of Shadrach's hutch. Three bags full! "Shadrach, Meshach, and Abed-we-go!"

His mind built the enormous picture of three big bags stacked in the barn, stuffed and round, piled one on top the other, piled so high they hid the little rabbit hutch that his father had made for him. That wonderful little rabbit hutch!

His father had known he couldn't wait that Saturday when he'd come home from Grandfather's farm to tell them all about Grandpa's great promise of a rabbit. His father had known he just couldn't wait for a hutch, even though the little black rabbit wasn't coming for a week.

"I guess you and I had better get right to that carpenter shop," Father had said, "and build that hutch right now. Being a good carpenter—if I say so myself—it won't take me long to slap a rabbit hutch together, but if I don't make it I'm afraid you'll fly to pieces. And how will I put you together again? I'm not *that* good a carpenter!"

That had been a wonderfully funny picture—he, Davie, flying to pieces. His father nailing him together again. With a crosspiece here and a plaster lath there and a few little nails, just to hold him together until the little rabbit came! He laughed aloud in the bed. Laughed his love for his rabbit and the little hutch and his father. "Shadrach, Meshach and Abed-we-go." That's why he had named the rabbit Shadrach.

Grandma heard him. "What did you say, Davie?"

"I said, 'Shadrach, Meshach and Abed-we-go.'" He wanted to tell Grandma how he had named the little rabbit that was coming Shadrach after the Abed-we-go game, but he was half afraid that if he got to telling about Shadrach, Meshach and Abed-we-go, he'd tell about the big plan for getting three bags of clover. It would just come out.

"Oh," Grandma said, but her mind was on the stove. "I started the potatoes too soon," Grandmother was telling him now. "Your grandfather is forgetting to come home again. The coffee will be tar. And I suppose he'll also forget to bring me a bunch of leaf lettuce."

As Grandma was saying that, there came Grandfather's heavy tread down the hall. The door opened, and it was just as if Grandpa had heard. "I'm late," he said, "but I didn't forget your lettuce." He carried the lettuce to Grandmother as if the lettuce were roses. Grandmother look annoyed, but Davie had to snicker in the bed.

Grandfather looked up at the bed in complete surprise. "And what's this fellow doing, slopping around in a lazy bed this bright and sunny day?" he asked Grandma.

"Yes, you and your promises," Grandmother

said. "Now he lives in that damp dark barn with that rabbit hutch. Even sneaked out of bed, mind you, while I was nodding for a minute over my knitting. I don't know why you didn't keep your promise to yourself and let the rabbit come as a surprise.
How Davie will ever get through this week —you and your promises!"

The potatoes suddenly sizzled louder, a loud harsh sound. Smoky steam rose up. With a vexed sound Grandma whirled to the stove. "There! And me standing there scolding. Now you've made me burn the potatoes!"

Behind Grandmother's back Grandpa winked. Davie winked back from the bed, although he had to screw up the whole side of his face to do it and his other eye went completely shut. Grandfather laughed.

Why, that's what he'd do if he had to go to bed every afternoon like a baby. He'd practice winking in bed, so he wouldn't have to screw up his whole face and close his other eye. That's what he'd do, except of course tomorrow. Tomorrow he was going to gather three whole bags of clover for his rabbit. Shadrach, Meshach and Abed-we-go!

"Grandpa," he suddenly asked from the bed, "are you allowed to pull up clover for a rabbit along the road? I know where there's a big patch."

"Why, of course," Grandfather said. "Along the road—that's public domain."

Public domain! He rolled it over in his mouth. Get clover for Shadrach from the public domain. Three bags full from the public domain. Shadrach, Meshach and Abed-we-go! It sounded big and tremendous. It would be a job! Tomorrow he'd do it.

He let himself slide out of bed. "Oh, I'm hungry all of a sudden," he told Grandma eagerly.

"Yes, and your grandfather made me burn the potatoes. Coals, that's what they are. Black coals! And the coffee is tar!"

Grandpa grinned.

CHAPTER 3

Only yesterday he'd made his big plan to gather three bags full of clover for Shadrach. And here he was, and here was the clover—his wooden shoes were touching it. It was a big patch! It stretched along between the road and the ditch. It was tall red clover, and it was full of blossoms and of bees. He hadn't expected bees. Well, he wasn't scared of bees. . . . But he was all alone here way outside the village. It must be a mile! The village tower rose far away. There was nobody nearby in any field. The empty gravel road stretched on below the dike. The whole dike was empty. There wasn't one sheep.

He looked at the clover again. It wouldn't be stealing! Grandpa had said it would be all right. But he wished there was somebody near. If somebody was near and didn't stop him from taking the clover, then he'd know it would be all right.

"Public domain," he said aloud to himself. If any of his playmates back there in the village would come to the house and ask Mother "Where's Davie?" Mother could say: "Oh, Davie went way out the village to get some clover for his rabbit along the public domain."

He laughed a little. That sounded big and important. Only—Mother didn't know. Nobody knew. His mother couldn't say that, because she didn't know he was here. Even Grandmother didn't know. It made him feel uneasy, alone. There wasn't a sound here, except the bees. The bees grumbled so. He quickly turned around to look at the village. The village tower rose there far away in the sky. He could see the big blank white face of the clock; it was almost like one big eye. Somehow the tower pointing up so still and straight seemed to threaten things.

That's where Mother and Grandmother were, back there where the tower rose. But they didn't know he was here. He'd sneaked out of

28

bed again. Oh, it had been easy. The moment Grandma had fallen asleep he'd just slid out of the bed, put on his clothes, and tiptoed out of the house. But he'd streaked to the barn. He'd grabbed three sacks, and then he'd found some string—just as easy—he'd hardly had to hunt at all.

Now here he was. The string was in his pocket, the empty sacks under his arm, and he'd thought of everything. But he hadn't thought of bees. The clover was thick with bees, small bright buzzing yellow bees, and all kinds of dark heavy rumbling bumblebees. They were all busy.

He laid his three sacks in a neat, careful row, but he didn't start to gather clover. It was so quiet here. The big tower stood there in the distance so still and straight and threatening. The big white eye of the clock didn't move, it seemed to be staring. Maybe he'd better pick up the sacks and run home and crawl back into bed again before Grandma woke up. She wouldn't like it if she found out he'd sneaked away again. He'd sneaked out yesterday, too.

But he turned his back on the tower and the clock. Without looking he stretched out his hand as far as he could reach and then snatched a quick handful of clover. The bees droned and kept busy—they didn't seem to mind. A little scared and shaky he edged up to the clover again, snatched another handful. The bees still didn't mind. He stuffed the two handfuls down in the sack. It made a little lump way down in a bottom corner of the bag. He felt the little lump. It was going to be a job. Three bags full! Oh, it would be a work!

He squeezed the little lump in the bottom of the sack again. It made him eager to begin to work, gather more. He dropped to his knees before the clover patch. But now the bees were close and big, right on a level with his eyes. They rumbled.

He carefully reached for a handful of clover, but kept his face half averted. Just as he was going to snatch the clover away, a big bumblebee came to land on one of the blossoms. He jerked his hand back, sat back on his heels, little scared chills going up and down his spine. But he managed to tell the bumblebee in a nice kind low voice: "You can have that clump, there's plenty." He reached for another clump far away from the bee. "I'll take this one," he explained to the bee, "but you can have that one. There's plenty." The bee didn't seem to mind.

Talking to the bee made him feel better, more sure of himself. He ripped some more clover away, but now he kept talking, kept promising the bees: "I won't hurt you." And if a bee came too close, he'd be careful to tell him: "There's plenty."

While he talked he tore at the clover as fast as he dared, and stuffed it in the sack. The first sack was beginning to fill. He wasn't scared of the bees any more, well, hardly. . . .

He crawled with his sack to the edge of the ditch. He peered over the bank. It was a deep ditch, and the whole steep ditch bank was covered with clover. It was dark and shadowy along the ditch, not sunny like the roadside. Down the dark bank there were hardly any bees.

The first sack was too full to take down the steep bank. He hurried to get the second one. With the empty sack he let himself slide flat on his stomach down the ditchside. He found toe holds and worked along the steep side of the ditch, filling his sack as he went. But the stuffed sack got clumsy, and then it got in his way, and when he tried to climb over it he slipped. Both his feet shot down and plopped into the water with a big cold splash. His wooden shoes filled. He gasped—it was such a shock and a scare—

and grabbed blindly for a big clump of clover.

There was a bee in the clover clump. The bee got caught when he suddenly grabbed and squeezed the clump of clover together. Under his hand the big bumblebee roared, it rattled among the clover stalks. Queer, scared tinglings

raced through his hand, but he clung, he didn't dare let go, and he pulled himself up by the clump of clover. As he pulled his feet out of the water the whole clump tore away from its roots, came away, was loose in his hand. He laughed a squeaky, scared laugh, but he had a toe hold now and he kept scrambling up the bank. He flung the bee and the clover far away from him.

He was safely up on the bank, but little cold scared shivers still ran through him. And now he was so scared of the ditch that he hardly dared to go after his sack. He threw himself down flat on the ground and reached down as far as he could. He could just grab the sack and pull it up. But as he drew the sack over the bank, he saw the bee. He had thrown the bee into the water with the handful of clover. It was clinging to a clover stalk. The big bee was so heavy that the stalk went under, but still the bee clung to it. The stalk floated away with the bee under water.

The bee was going to drown, and he had thrown the bee into the water. It made him feel bad. It worried him—now all the bees might get mad at him, even though he hadn't done it on purpose. The stalk was floating away. The bee kept crawling and crawling along the stalk under the water. He ought to save the bee! But he didn't know how to save a bee. He walked along the ditch, following the floating stalk, searching for a stick or a piece of wood. He couldn't find any.

Then he thought of his wooden shoe. He jerked the shoe off one foot and let it slide down the steep bank right at the bee. The shoe hit the water, slid over it, and bumped the stalk of clover. And after a moment—there came the wet, bedraggled bee crawling up the wooden shoe. It crawled to the very tippety point of the shoe and there it sat, squashed and pasty. Oh, it was a big one, it must be a grandfather bumblebee. But now it wasn't a bee, now it was Noah in the ark, floating down the current of the ditch on his wooden shoe. Davie laughed at the thought and felt good about the bee.

The shoe floated along, and the bee sat very still and frumpled and wet. Suddenly it stirred and then it began drying itself furiously. It whirred its wings, it wiped its face with all kinds of legs, it twirled its rump in a fast little circle to get itself dry. In no time the half-drowned bee was dry. In no time it spread its wings and zoomed up, straight up from the shoe, straight at him! The big bee rumbled about his head. He stumbled back, his eyes up toward the bee. "But I saved you," he stammered. "And I didn't mean to throw you in the water."

The bee was circling to get its bearings—the bee wasn't angry with him. Suddenly it knew where it wanted to go, and with an extra loud roar it shot high into the sky and zoomed away.

Oh, what a relief. He stood there watching the bee out of sight, and long after, until all the scare had slowly eased away. Then he suddenly missed his wooden shoe. It wasn't there. It had gone sailing on, it was far down the ditch. He chased it, looking desperately for a stick. Suddenly he realized that the shoe was floating away because the ditch had a current. But that meant that this was a *draught* ditch! Other ditches emptied into this ditch, but this ditch went to the canal, and the canal went to the sea. Mother had always warned him against getting near drainage ditches, but especially draught ditches because they were really deep and had a current. And here he'd been gathering clover right down the bank of a draught ditch; his feet had even gone down into it! It scared him now. He looked back at the tower with the white face of the clock in the town where his mother was. The big eye was staring.

He looked desperately after his shoe sailing away. And then he saw a stick! He raced after the shoe, passed it, threw himself down flat. He could just poke the end of the stick into the toe of his shoe as it came sailing along. Triumphantly he lifted the shoe out of the water. He felt much better now. He shoved his wet foot into the wet shoe and hurried back to the clover patch.

Everything was all right now. He hadn't gone down in the ditch, and his shoe hadn't floated away. He looked out over the empty fields where the canal must be. Imagine his wooden shoe going down the canal and into the sea and sailing way over the sea, way to America. The people in America would pick up the shoe and look at it and say: "Oh, look, here's Davie's shoe. Davie must have drowned!"

It gave him cold shivers, he in the ditch drowned, his shoe sailing on to America. Only —he quickly reassured himself—no one, why, no one, knew about him in America. They didn't even know his name! It was just all scary make believe. He looked at the distant tower for reassurance, but the tower looked even more threatening, for now there were clouds around it, and the sun had gone away, and the white eye of the clock seemed to stare out of the clouds.

He hastily decided to put the clover in little piles, then he'd just drag the last sack along and push the piles into the sack. He really had to hurry now if he was going to get back before Grandma woke up. The cloudiness and the shadowy land worried him. He kept away from the ditch, kept his eyes away from the clock in the tower.

A little later he glanced back at his little piles of clover. Oh boy, soon he'd have three bags full. Three bags full for his little black rabbit. Shadrach, he decided, was the first sack. The second sack was Meshach, and the one he still had to fill was going to be Abed-we-go. He tried to make a little inside song of it. It wouldn't sing. He was too anxious deep down inside. He wished the sun would come from behind the clouds.

Then there was hard running down the road. Somebody came running hard. It was his brother, Rem! Something was wrong. He sat scared still for a moment, but then he started tearing at the clover with both hands as fast as he could, crawling faster and faster, as if he were running away from Rem. He just had to have enough clover for the last sack before Rem stopped him. He knew Rem would stop him.

"Where have you been all afternoon?" Rem was shouting down the road. "Everybody's out looking for you, and Mother's crying."

He tore at the clover without answering Rem, faster, faster. . . . Now Rem was standing over him. "Are you going to catch it! Know what

37

time it is? Six o'clock almost. Grandpa and Dad and even Grandma are all out looking for you. And Mother's asking everyone coming home from the fields if they've seen you, and nobody has, and she's crying. She's sure you drowned in a ditch."

He looked quickly up at Rem to see if what Rem was saying was really true, but Rem was looking at the bags and all the little piles of clover. "What do you think you're doing anyway?"

"Getting clover for my rabbit."

"Two bags full for one little rabbit? Man, that's enough for a cow!"

"Three bags full," he said stoutly. "Rem," he begged, "will you help me put these piles in the sack and tie them up, then we can quick carry them home."

"But your rabbit isn't coming till Saturday!"

"I know," he said. He couldn't explain to Rem that he'd just had to do something for his little rabbit, and that the three bags had seemed such a wonderful plan. Rem would laugh.

"But didn't you know that all that green clover will spoil? It'll be one rotten mess by Saturday. Besides rabbits can't eat tall red clover— short white clover is all right, but red clover makes them bloat. Why, your rabbit would blow up like a balloon."

He stared at Rem in dismay. "Honest, Rem?" He didn't want to believe it.

"Honest!" Rem said. "He'd blow up like a balloon from that red clover. And there he'd go —straight up in the sky. Way up, just as high as that skylark singing there." Rem pointed to a skylark hanging high in the sky, singing its evening song. "Way up there he'd go, and then— *bang*—he'd burst into a thousand little pieces. *Bang!*—just like that."

It wasn't so! He wouldn't believe it! He wasn't going to believe it! But just the same it had him staring up in the sky at that dot of a skylark. The skylark being there somehow made it so real and true, almost as if it *were* happening. It wasn't so! Rem was pestering and teasing again, just to make him so mad that he'd cry. He wasn't going to cry! But Rem sounded so sure.

"Man, didn't you even know about bloat?" Rem was saying.

No, he didn't know about bloat. Why did Rem always have to pester?

"It's really so," Rem said. "Rabbits can't eat tall red clover. Why, he'd bloat up and then he'd blow up, and there would come the little pieces falling from the sky. A piece of fur, and then a piece of a leg, a tail, and then a couple of ears . . ."

Right then and there he jumped up and hit Rem. Hit him and hit him with his fists, and all the time he was hitting he was crying, but he was crying because he was so mad, so mad. Hit him and cry, hit him and cry. . . . But he helplessly had to let his hands fall. Rem just stood there laughing and holding him off.

"Instead of hitting me you ought to be thankful," Rem said in that pestering voice. "Here I'm saving your rabbit from bursting, and you want to hit me. Suppose I'd just let you feed him that clover?"

Then Rem kicked one of the piles of clover into the ditch.

"NO!" he yelled. "NO!" He almost pushed Rem backward into the draught ditch right then. He wanted to, even if it was a draught ditch with a current! But it scared him when Rem stumbled backward over one of the bags, it scared him so that his angry crying stopped dead in his mouth. Rem managed to catch his balance, and then Rem suddenly stopped pestering and became the good brother he could be,

40

not teasing. It was such an immense relief it almost made him cry again.

"Honest, Davie, we might just as well throw it in the ditch, it'll spoil anyway." Rem said in a new, chummy voice, "but if you want it so bad . . ." Rem started to scrape up all the piles of clover with him and even tied up the sacks for him. Then Rem slammed one of the soft round sacks down on his shoulders. "Put your hand way up against your side," Rem told him, "that makes your shoulder wider so the sack won't roll off."

Rem put two big bags on his own shoulder. Together they went shouldering down the road with bags on their backs, like big men. He felt big and proud, going down the road with Rem, even though he was really anxious now about Mother and Grandmother, and about sneaking out of bed again. Just then the clock in the far away tower bonged.

"Do you know what time that is?" Rem asked.

"No."

"Well, it's six o'clock, so you've been gone three hours. Dad and Grandpa and everybody's out looking for you. Didn't you even look at the clock in the tower?"

"I can't tell time," he had to admit to Rem.

41

Rem knew that! "Are they crying?" he asked hastily.

"Who? Dad and Grandpa?"

Rem was going to start teasing again, but just then he happened to notice Davie's feet. "How'd you get wet feet?"

"Oh, there was a lot of nice clover down the bank, and I slipped."

It looked as if that scared Rem! And Mother always said that nothing scared Rem, and she wished it would, then he wouldn't be so reckless.

"Suppose you'd slipped in and drowned?" Rem said.

"I didn't slip in—only my feet," he said stoutly, because now he was a little scared himself, if Rem was scared.

Rem whistled. "Whew, and you just through being sick. If Mom sees those wet feet, she'll keep you in bed for a week instead of just afternoons." Rem threw down his sacks and made him sit down on his own sack. "Here stick out your feet." Rem pulled his shoes and socks off. He wrung the socks so hard that they squeaked in his hands and then flapped them around in the air to dry them some more. He even wiped out the wooden shoes with his handkerchief.

It made the handkerchief a mess, but Rem

didn't seem to care, he just shoved it deep down in his pocket. "I always catch it for something, anyway," he said.

Rem inspected the inside of the wooden shoes. "There, they look pretty good. Maybe now she won't notice, and then she won't feel your socks and find out they're wet. You wouldn't want to go to bed for a week, would you?"

"NO! I hate bed!"

"Me, too," Rem said.

Oh, Rem could be a good brother. Just then a piece of thistledown happened to come floating along, and it caught in Rem's red hair. He pointed to it and told Rem. Rem picked it out of his hair and looked at it. "Look at that," he said, "still fur from your rabbit floating down."

They laughed and laughed. Now it was a good joke, and he could laugh about it. But just

the same he told Rem: "My rabbit's going to be
black, and that's white."

They didn't talk the last part of the way. He
was getting really scared the closer they came to
home. When at last they turned into Grandfather's yard with their sacks, his heart sank, for
there they all were in the yard. All four—

Grandpa, Grandma, Mother, Dad. All four
standing there, just looking at him. And just
like that Rem changed. He walked a little faster
out ahead, and he yelled out: "Just look at this
—went out and worked three hours to get three
bags of clover for one little rabbit." Rem tried
to sound like a grown-up, and he threw his two
bags down hard in the yard.

He stood there scared before them all. But

when he looked up, to his utter amazement they all were laughing about the three big bags of clover for one little rabbit. They weren't angry —even Father laughed. They all laughed except Mother. She stayed worried, and she just looked at him. Then suddenly she stepped forward and stooped and felt his socks.

"Oh," Rem said awfully loud and quick, "when I found him he'd got his shoes all messed up with clay, I washed them in a ditch, but there wasn't time to dry them."

Over his mother's stooped back he looked in open-mouthed amazement at his big brother. Rem had lied for him! It made him feel so queer deep down inside that he hastily decided he'd tell his mother the truth. Not today! But some day.

Grandma was looking at the bags as if she couldn't believe it. "My, oh my, oh my, Davie— did you gather all that clover?"

"He's a little worker," Grandpa said. Grandpa sounded proud of him.

"You spoil him," Father said to Grandpa, and now his voice was stern. "Do you know you were gone three hours, Davie? And they tell me you've sneaked out of bed two days in a row."

He had no answer, and Mother still looked

worried, but Grandpa gathered up all three bags and carried them to the barn—all three at once. Then Rem said in his grown-up voice: "I told him the clover would spoil long before the rabbit came, and even if it didn't, it would bloat the little rabbit. Isn't that so, Grandpa?"

But Grandpa didn't bother to answer Rem. He just walked away with the three sacks.

"I told him it was no use bringing it home," Rem said to the other grown-ups. "But he had to bring it home."

"Of course, he had to bring it home after working like that," Grandpa said over his shoulder to Rem.

But Grandma looked at the three big bags Grandpa was carrying, and she said: "What's it going to be, Davie? Three bags for the rabbit a week too soon, but after you've had him for a week the poor little animal can grunt from hunger?"

It wasn't nice of Grandma to say that, but then he'd sneaked out of bed twice and worried her. Now everybody laughed at him again because of what Grandma had said.

Rabbits didn't grunt, anyway! And Grandpa was proud of him!

CHAPTER 4

He was being punished! Mother was punishing him in the worst way she could possibly punish him—by keeping him from going to Grandpa's barn. He had to stay in the house. The three bags with clover must be lying just where Grandpa had dropped them. Wherever that was. He didn't know. He hoped Grandpa had stacked them one on top of the other right in front of Shadrach's hutch, because that was exactly what he'd planned to do. But he hadn't had a chance. Mother had taken him right straight home, the moment Grandpa had gone into the barn with the three bags.

He'd had to stay in the house all day yesterday, too! And from now on he was going to have to sleep in their own house every afternoon—no more sleeping at Grandma's.

"Oh, no, that's done," Mother had told him yesterday. "You sneaking out of bed and even out of the village! You take advantage of your nice Grandma. And that's not exactly the nicest thing to do."

He knew that! But he didn't know how to explain to Mother that it wasn't really sneaking, because he hadn't *meant* it to be sneaking. He'd simply had to do it because three bags full for Shadrach had been such a wonderful big plan. He did tell Mother that he'd planned to stay in bed every afternoon all the rest of the week until Shadrach came, even if Grandmother did fall asleep. All Mother had said was: "I'm supposed to believe that after you sneaked out twice?"

And he'd told her: "Yes, honest, Mother—because I was going to practice winking." That hadn't been the smartest thing to say.

All day yesterday in the house! He certainly hadn't expected that Tuesday night when Mother'd taken him straight home. Oh, she had made him go to bed. But not without supper—the way she did with Rem—and going to bed with your supper wasn't much punishment.

She'd put him to bed with his feet wrapped in a prickly woolen shawl. But that was just fussy, it wasn't really punishment, it was just because Mother worried so because his feet had been wet and he was just over being sick.

All day yesterday—that was Wednesday—she'd kept him in the house. The whole day in the house, and the whole long afternoon, way until supper time, in bed. And she'd closed the doors of the closet bed almost shut. "And don't you practice winking," she'd said. "Winking isn't sleeping."

In the dark in the bed it had been the longest afternoon in all time, in all the world.

But now it was gone, the whole horrible Wednesday. Now it was Thursday morning, and he'd already added Wednesday to Monday and Tuesday and put them away—those three waiting days were gone. Now there were only Thursday, Friday and part of Saturday to wait for the little black rabbit.

But here it was Thursday morning, and it looked like he was going to have to stay in the house all day again! It didn't seem possible, but it looked like it. He'd already teased almost all he dared. It hadn't done a bit of good, but he had to try once more. "Mom," he said just off-hand, "may I run out to Grandma a minute—just to see Grandma?"

Mother didn't even consider it. "No, I can't trust you. You'd no doubt run away again and get wet feet again."

Every time she said that about his wet feet! Every time, it gave him a queer low feeling down deep in his stomach.

He eyed his mother, puzzling what to do. He slipped from behind the table then and almost went to her to tell her that he'd got his feet wet because he'd gone into the ditch. But that would be telling that Rem had lied! It didn't seem right after Rem had been such a good brother, the best ever. It would really scare Mother that he'd been in the ditch. And Rem would catch it. It stopped him.

No, later he'd tell Mother the truth. Later—oh, when he was as big as Rem. No, he wouldn't wait that long. Some day he'd go up to Mother and say: "Mom, remember when I was little and sneaked away to get three bags of clover for my rabbit? Well, I slid in the ditch and got my feet wet. It was a draught ditch, too!" No, he wouldn't tell her that it was a draught ditch, not even then. It would scare Mother too much.

He had to hang on to that plan. He even had

50

to put himself behind the table again and sit quietly and as far out of sight as possible, because his tongue kept feeling as if he was going to tell Mother in spite of everything. He stared hard at the old alarm clock on the table and twiddled with the hands, but he had to watch himself all the time. He wanted so badly to make everything right with Mother, and get out of the house again.

He held it back somehow, but it was hard. He had to watch himself all the time, otherwise his mouth would be saying the words. He couldn't even think about Shadrach and the clover. He was worried about the clover, and what Rem had said—that the clover would spoil, and that if Shadrach ate it he'd blow up and burst. Rem had tried to sound like a big man, he decided spitefully. "Won't it spoil, Grandpa? And won't rabbits bloat from eating red clover?" he said half aloud in the room, imitating Rem. Mother was dusting, but now she turned and looked at him. She must have heard him mumbling to himself. He hastily twirled the hands of the old alarm clock.

Grandpa hadn't answered Rem one word. He wished he could have asked Grandpa if the clover would spoil and if Shadrach would blow

up and burst from eating it. But there hadn't
been a chance—Mother had taken him straight
home.

Mother was still dusting the room. He waited
until she looked up. "Mother," he started.

But Mother just said: "Davie, you've asked
me seventeen times already. And seventeen
times I've told you I don't know anything about
clover and bloat. You'll have to ask Grandpa."

"But you won't let me go to Grandpa's," he
whined. He hadn't meant to whine, but that was
the way it came out.

"That's right," Mother said, and got very
busy with her dusting. But then she looked at
him again. "How are you coming with that
clock?"

"Oh, fine," he said quickly and very loudly,
because he wasn't sure at all. It seemed he'd sat
all morning with the old alarm clock that didn't
have any glass on its face—trying to learn to tell
time. He hadn't really given his mind to it, he'd
just sat twirling the hands to make his mother
think he was trying hard, but he'd really been
worrying about the clover. Rem had said it
would rot!

He made a quick decision, jumped up from
the table and hurried to his mother with the

clock. He twirled the big hand with his finger and set the hands for a quarter after nine—he hoped. Maybe if he did it really well now, Mother would let him go for just one quick look at the clover. "This is a quarter after nine," he told Mother. He turned the big hand around the dial. "But this is a quarter to three." He gave the hands another quick twirl. "And this is a quarter after twelve." A last fast twirl. "But this is three o'clock. Right on the dot!" He had made it sound very sure, much surer than he felt. He looked at his mother.

His mother smiled a little, and he drew a big breath. Now Mother would take the clock, he knew, but now he wasn't worried. Those four places he had moved the hands to himself were the ones that always got him mixed up. Now Mother could move the hands any old place, he'd know! He stood ready, eager, sure. Mother changed the hands, but every time in a sure, loud voice he told her exactly what time it was. Mother looked proud of him, even though she didn't say so out loud. "Well," she said at last, "now when you run away you'll at least know what time it is. Although I hope you'll never do it again."

"Oh, no, Mother, never!" he said. He pleaded

with his eyes for her to believe him. Then he said quickly: "Mom, may I run over to Grandma's quick a minute and show Grandma how I can tell time?" He reached out his hand for the clock.

Mother held the clock a minute. Then she said: "Well, all right, I guess. You'd just lie wide awake in bed all afternoon, worrying about that clover instead of sleeping. And in bed we sleep." She showed him the clock and moved the hands. "Look, now that you can tell time, it's *this* time now. I'm giving you fifteen minutes, but I'm adding every minute that you are gone over those fifteen to your sleeping time. So in a way it really makes no difference how long you are gone, because it's just going to be added to the other end of your sleeping time—even if you have to stay in bed all through supper, without supper. Understand?"

He nodded. He looked up at his mother in some surprise. It sounded fierce.

"That's fair, isn't it?" Mother said.

He nodded again.

"All right, Mother," he said in a little voice, then he grabbed the clock and ran. But he dashed right back down the hall, jumped up and hugged his mother so hard with the clock

54

in his hand that the clock hurt her. If the clock
hadn't got in his way, he would have kissed her,
too. But now that he had hurt her it somehow
made him think of his wet feet. And now he

couldn't kiss her. "I'll be right back, Mother,"
he promised. He stormed out of the house.

Grandma was sitting in the reed chair at the
window, nodding, so he didn't bother her. Instead he slipped into the barn, set the clock
down on the floor, and hurried to the sacks.

Grandpa hadn't piled them up—he'd just dropped them. Davie decided he would just quick pile them up, stack them one on top of the other right in front of the little hutch the way he had planned to do it, just to see how it would look. Then he'd quick show Grandma how he could tell time, and then he'd run right home again.

He picked up the first sack with clover, but as he lugged it to the hutch it seemed to feel warm and damp in his hands. There was a queer sweet hot smell that seemed to come from the sack. He untied Rem's knot and poked his hand inside. The clover was hot inside the sack. His hand came out sticky—smelly hot. He hurried to the other sacks and ripped them open. Rem had said the clover would be one rotten mess. It was! All the clover had spoiled. All three bags!

He stood in utter dismay among the opened bags. Grandpa hadn't said a thing about the clover spoiling! Not a thing—he hadn't even bothered to answer Rem.

He stood bewildered. He felt sick. Now the bad smell was all through the barn. Why hadn't Grandpa told him the clover would spoil. He would have believed Grandpa! But Grandpa had even carried it into the barn for him.

This he could not understand. He stood in sick dismay. The bad, spoiled smell coming out of the bags hung thick and heavy in the barn. He retched.

He had to hurry to the door, open it for air. He was sick. He sat down flat in the doorway where the fresh air was. He had to sit down, had to work this out for himself, this thing about Grandpa. And then he thought he knew. Grandpa hadn't said a word, because Grandpa had been proud of him for all that hard work. That was it! Grandpa had even told Rem: "Of course he had to bring it home after working so hard." Now he knew. Grandpa just hadn't wanted to tell him right out before Rem that the clover would spoil. That was it! That must be it.

Everything eased in him. He brightened. He jumped up and looked back at the three sacks. He came to a quick decision, made a quick plan. They'd all laughed at him for getting three bags of clover for one tiny rabbit, and Rem had said it would spoil. How Rem would laugh now! Well, he'd bury it!

He dashed back into the barn, grabbed two of the sacks with clover. He kept watching the window and Grandma as he dragged the sacks across the yard to Grandpa's compost pile. He raced back after the last sack and a pitchfork. Now if Grandma just slept a little longer, nobody would ever know. They had all laughed about his three sacks with clover, but they'd never know. He'd bury it way down deep in Grandpa's compost pile. If only Grandma just kept sleeping a little longer.

He struggled the sacks with clover to the top of the compost pile in the far corner of the yard. He threw the pitchfork up and climbed up after it. He raked away the top layer of covering straw, digging away with the unwieldy fork. Soon he'd be done, then nobody could laugh, nobody would know.

Setting his teeth hard against the stench, he shook the first two bags empty into the deep hole he'd dug in the middle of the compost pile. But he hadn't dug the hole big enough—the clover wouldn't all go in. He jumped on it, trampled it. It wouldn't even trample in, and it stuck messily to his scrubbed wooden shoes, staining them all green and juicy. The sweet sick odors rose. He gagged so loudly that he looked hastily at Grandmother's window to see if she had heard.

He was desperate. There was a whole sackful still to go in, and it wouldn't go in. He thought of pulling the straw over it, but that would leave a big camel hump right in the middle of Grandpa's compost pile. Grandpa would see it right away. Grandpa kept his compost pile as flat and neat as a tablecloth on a table. That's what Grandma always said. "You'd think it was a dining room table or a guest bed," she always said.

It wasn't funny now. He struggled with the big unhandy fork, half sick, teeth set, mouth tight against the sickly smell.

"DAVIE!"

He jumped.

It was Grandma. "Oh, Davie, now what? I woke up and there you were on top of the compost pile with a big sharp fork."

"Grandma," he said half crying with relief, "all my clover spoiled. Rem said it would! And

59

I've got to get right back for my afternoon nap, and I can't get it buried. Rem said it would be one big rotten mess, and that's what it is!"

Grandma understood at once. "And you don't want him laughing at you. You don't want anybody to know."

"Yes," he said helplessly. "Yes. But Grandpa will see the big bump."

"Here, help me up," Grandma ordered. "That big fork is too much for you to handle."

He had to reach out his hand, steady and pull Grandma up the slippery straw side of the compost pile. She took the fork from him. Oh, she was clever! She just spread a tuft of clover here, tucked a tuft of clover there—she spread out all the clover that was left, just as flat! And Grandma didn't even gag! Oh, it was clever. Now she pulled the straw back over, tucked it and patted it, and there was the compost pile as flat as ever. As flat and neat as a tablecloth! He stood to one side on the compost pile admiring and loving his grandmother.

."There," Grandmother said. "Now nobody but you and me will ever know. And nobody needs to know. It's a secret between you and me."

He wanted to kiss Grandmother right then

and there, but it didn't seem quite right to kiss your grandmother on top of a compost pile. Instead he worried how Grandma was going to get down, she was such an old, old lady. But Grandmother just sat down flat on the edge of the compost pile and let herself slide down the slippery straw. Oh, she was clever! He was so grateful that he took the pitchfork from her hand and dashed toward the barn with it.

"Davie, no!" Grandma shouted after him. "Don't run with that sharp fork. Here, let me take it to the barn." Obediently he brought the fork to her, but Grandma not only carried the fork. She even took the damp smelly sacks back to the barn, and she didn't gag at all!

There in the barn stood the forgotten alarm clock right in the middle of the earthen floor!

Grandma stared at the clock. "Oh," she said at last, "I see you carry a watch with you now."

He laughed and laughed with Grandma. What a big watch! But then he explained to Grandma that he had to be back home in fifteen minutes. Otherwise every extra minute would get added to his afternoon sleeping time, even if he had to stay in bed all through supper time without any supper. "Have I been here longer than fifteen minutes, Grandma?"

Grandma laughed. "Davie, I think you're going to be just like your grandfather—no sense of time. Why, you must have been here easily a half hour or more."

He sighed. "Then no supper," he said. But it really didn't make him feel bad at all. It didn't seem important, not now with the clover buried.

"Without supper, eh?" Grandma said. "In that case maybe we'd better reinforce you with a cookie."

They went to the house with the alarm clock. "Grandma," he carefully explained, "I'll have to show you how I can tell time some other time, and I'll have to tell Mother our secret, otherwise she'll maybe think I sneaked away again. But I didn't—I didn't even think of it."

"Oh, that's all right—to tell your mother our secrets," Grandma said. And though she'd said *a* cookie, she handed him a whole handful. Then she noticed his green-stained wooden shoes, and wouldn't let him go until she had scrubbed them white and clean. She did it slowly and carefully so the insides wouldn't get wet.

He went down the street slowly and carefully. He had to. With an alarm clock in one hand and too many cookies in the other hand, he couldn't run. Going so slowly took still more time to be added to his sleeping time, but he didn't care much now. They had a secret—Grandma and he, and Mother too after he told her. He decided he'd tell Mother this secret, be-  cause he couldn't tell her that other secret about slipping in the draught ditch—not yet, not for a long time yet. But Mother would understand that the clover just had to be buried.

He'd tell Mother, he'd give her a big kiss, and then he'd go straight to bed. If it had to be all through supper time, then it had to be. The clover was buried.

CHAPTER 5

Now it was Saturday. At last it was Saturday morning! But it was raining. Because it was raining, Grandfather had not gone out to his little truck farm but was tidying the barn. Davie was trying to help Grandpa, but he couldn't keep his mind on it. He kept worrying about the rain. The rain poured off the roof, it fell in sheets across the wide open doorway of the old barn, it gurgled and rattled and splashed up from the ground again.

"Grandfather?"

Grandpa was busy folding up sacks and stacking them in a neat pile. Now he was folding the three sacks in which the spoiled clover had been, but he didn't say anything about them, he just folded the dried-out sacks and smoothed them out.

"Grandfather?" he said again. Now Grandpa looked up. "Grandpa, if it rains this afternoon will Maartens come just the same with his china-ware wagon?"

"Oh, sure," Grandfather said. "Maartens always comes."

"But won't his dishes get all wet?"

"Not to speak of a little black rabbit getting all wet," Grandpa said, and he started to chuckle. But Grandpa saw his worried face. "It seems to me, Davie," Grandpa said slowly and loudly, to make himself heard above the splashing of the rain, "that Maartens was already carting dishes when I was a boy—or so it seems. And by this time Maartens knows all the tricks. He knows that no housewife would so much as take one look at his dishes if they were wet, and all sticky with straw chaff. So for rainy days Maartens has a covered wagon, and there are his dishes and his little rabbits, all snug and dry and cozy under the canvas of his covered wagon. And always Maartens comes on Saturdays—rain or shine. Always!"

"Oh," he said. "Oh."

It was good when Grandpa explained everything so carefully and clearly. When Grandpa got through there were no little questions left nagging on behind in his mind, and all he could say was "Oh"—it made him feel so good and satisfied.

"Grandpa," he said, "is it almost noon?"

"I'm afraid not, Davie. Not even almost." Grandpa looked at the rain splashing in the doorway. "But it will come, Davie. It'll come."

"Yes," he said and looked at the sack Grandpa was folding.

"Grandpa?" he said.

"Yes, Davie."

He hesitated. It was funny, but he just couldn't keep a secret from Grandpa. "Grandfather," he said carefully, "the clover did spoil —just like Rem said. It got hot and nasty. Grandma and I buried it in your compost pile."

"Well, thank you, Davie. Clover's very good stuff to have in a compost pile. And when you dig it into the soil, how it makes things grow!"

"Oh," he said, pleased that he had done right. "But, Grandpa," he asked carefully, "did you know the clover would spoil like Rem said?"

"I was afraid of it, Davie."

"But you didn't say anything, Grandpa. They

66

all laughed about the three big bags of clover, but you didn't say it would spoil."

"No, Davie, I was proud of you. Such a big job for a little man, and you carried it right through to the finish."

He glowed inside. Oh, he loved his grandfather! He came a little closer. "Grandpa, did you know, too, that rabbits would bloat and die from eating red clover? Rem said my rabbit would blow up like a balloon, and go up in the air as high as a lark, and then he'd burst into a thousand pieces."

"Ah, your big brother always makes things sound so bad and big," Grandpa said impatiently. "It wouldn't be so bad as all that."

"But did you know, Grandpa?" he persisted. He had to know for sure that Grandfather knew.

"Yes, Davie, I knew it wouldn't do his stomach one little bit of good."

"Oh, Grandpa," he said relieved. "Then I'm really glad it spoiled—all three bags."

"Well, but Davie! Do you think I'd have let you feed it to your little rabbit? I just wanted you to have the three bags of clover in the barn, because I knew it was helping you to wait for your rabbit."

Grandpa had known all the time! His eyes went moist with pleasure. Grandpa had let him keep the clover, but he wouldn't have let him feed it to Shadrach so the little rabbit would die. "Grandpa," he said confusedly. He didn't know what he'd been going to say. "Grandpa," he said again. Then because he still did not know what to say, he quickly made up a big promise, because he was so grateful. "Grandpa, next year we'll dig that spoiled clover into the bean patch, and I'll help you plant beans again, and . . . and . . ."

"Fine, Davie, fine. It'll make wonderful beans."

It still rained and it still was nowhere near noon, not even almost, Grandpa had said. The rain was monotonous and dreary and slow, and the morning was dreadful and dreary and long, but it was good to be with Grandpa in the barn.

"Grandpa?" he started to say, but he swallowed his words. "Grandfather, what time is it now?" he said softly inside of himself. The question kept coming to the end of his tongue. He could hear it inside himself, even before he said it aloud. He would pull the words back, then all of a sudden before he knew it he would be saying them out loud again: "Grandpa, what time is it now?"

"Child," Grandfather said, "it's just three minutes later from when you asked me last— if that much."

Grandpa was getting impatient with him now. He didn't sound impatient, but the words sounded impatient, even though Grandpa looked kind. Davie was sorry he had asked. He mustn't ask again. But the question was already coming to the end of his tongue. Already he could hear the words inside himself again. He mustn't ask!

Later—amidst all the slow, rainy dreariness of the long, slow morning—there came a big surprise! Grandpa was way back in the barn, moving a stack of crates. All of a sudden there from behind those crates a door appeared! He hadn't known a door was there. He hurried over to his grandfather. Grandpa was tugging the door open. And the door let into another barn!

No, it wasn't another barn but a big square room, with windows. The windows were all boarded up, and it was very dark in the room— dark and dusty and cob-webby.

Grandpa went through the door into the room. He followed close behind. "Oh, Grandpa, I never knew there was a room back here!"

"You didn't!" Grandpa said. "Well, I thought I'd told you. You certainly must have heard me talk about my old school—the one I went to when I was a boy like you? Well, this is my old school!"

"The school you went to when you were a little boy?" he asked astounded. It seemed unbelievable. It seemed hundreds of years ago.

"Yes," Grandpa said. "And right there is where I sat." He pointed to a corner. "That is where my seat was."

It was unbelievable. He couldn't get his mind around it. Imagine Grandpa sitting in this school. Imagine Grandpa later buying his own school when he got old! But it didn't look like a school now—it was just a big dusty dark room.

"I never knew it was here," he said in awed unbelief. "You can't tell from outside that it's here. It just looks like part of the barn."

"That's the way I built the barn," Grandpa said. "Right tight against my old school. Yes, this really was my old school, and that's where I sat." Grandpa chuckled. "Can't believe it, can you? But Davie, there—over there near that last window—that is where your mother sat when she was a girl."

"And Dad, where did he sit?" he asked eagerly. "Right behind Mother?"

"No, I don't think your father went to this school," Grandpa said. "I don't believe he did."

It was a bit of a disappointment. Imagine Grandpa, and then later Mother also when she was a little girl—maybe with pigtails, even. "Grandpa," he said. "I didn't know. I didn't even know the door was there. You've never opened it before. You never come here."

"No," Grandpa said, "not any more. But this used to be a busy place. I used to keep all my fishing gear in here when I was still a fisherman out on the seas. Then when I got too old for that and got to be a canal boat man, going from town to town down all the canals, I kept all the boat stuff in here. But when I got to be really old, then I just bought me a little truck garden, and now I don't need this room any more. The barn is big enough."

"Oh," he said, and tried to put his mind around all the years that Grandpa had done all those things. It seemed hundreds of years ago. "And now you never come here any more," he said softly.

"Well, I'll tell you, Davie. I never come here any more, because it makes me a little bit sad— the ships I used to sail, the fish I used to catch, the boats I had." Grandpa pointed to the back wall where it was really dark. There against the wall, reaching up to the ceiling, stood a huge ship's rudder. Right in front of the rudder lay a great rusty sea anchor. There were other smaller anchors, and folded sails and nets, and crates, and barrels, and all kinds of piled up gear. Why, there was even the mast of a canal boat. It rose up out of the middle of a pile of

72

poles with big flat knobs on their ends. He knew what those were! Those were the poles the men on the canal boats used to push the boats along when the wind died down. They put the flat knobs against their chests, and pushed and pushed. "Oh, look at all the boat poles," he gasped. "And the anchor and the mighty rudder. I never knew all this was here."

"It is mighty, isn't it?" Grandfather said. He rubbed his hand softly over the big rudder, just as if it were a dog or a horse.

"No, I don't come here any more," Grandpa said. "But I thought today I'd show it to you to take your mind off the little rabbit, and give you something to do." Grandpa patted his shoulder. "Well, I'll be out there tidying up the barn, but you play in here as long as you like."

Now he was all alone in the big, secret room. Step by step he backed away from the huge, looming rudder, step by step until he stood in the middle of the room. It was quiet and dark here, dusty and old. The rain sounded dimly on the roof. He could just hear Grandpa making small noises as he worked in the outer barn. Oh, it was quiet. The thick dust made everything silent here. It all stood there, so still and old and dusty. It scared him a little—the dim, silent room, the quiet huge things looming there against the black wall. He was ashamed. Grandpa had made this big surprise especially for him, and he wasn't even playing, just standing, just scared.

He widened his eyes and tried to imagine all kinds of big things he could do. Why, he could climb way up on that rudder, and sit up there and make believe the rudder was a big fishing ship. Down below, the floor would be so far away it would look like a sea. But he did not move toward the hulking rudder. Instead he stood listening for sounds from Grándpa. He did not hear a thing, he started edging toward the door.

But then there was a slight noise in the outer barn, and he made himself stop. Why, he could pull down some of the crates, and put them behind each other on the floor and make believe it was a canal boat. Then he could push with one of the canal boat poles, and make believe he was going from town to town down all the canals all over the country. He could even crawl behind and under all that stuff and explore—there were all kinds of little tunnels and passages. That would be fun! And nobody would know he was here, because nobody knew the secret room was here. He could play and explore for hours. Nobody would know.

He edged a little closer to the door. Everything was so silent in the dust. So old and long ago. It was just as if today wasn't today! As if the little rabbit wasn't really coming. It was a queer feeling. But Shadrach was coming today! Now he didn't hear Grandpa at all. He edged still a little closer to the door, and promised himself very hard that some day he'd come here and play. Play and play, climb and explore, and crawl behind everything and . . . and . . . He pelted from the room, out through the door and into the outer barn.

Grandpa was there, Grandpa had been there all the time. Grandpa was busy, the rain was splashing in the open doorway, Grandpa did not notice him. He didn't know what to do—

Grandpa had especially opened the room for him and told him to play, and here he'd come running right out, he hadn't played at all. At last Grandpa looked up. He looked surprised. "Through so soon?"

He nodded his head, miserable and unhappy. He did not know what to say. Grandpa must be terribly disappointed with him. He wanted badly to ask if he might play in the hidden room some other day, but it didn't seem right to ask that after Grandpa had opened up the room for him and he'd done nothing with it. He felt wretched. He was glad Grandpa got busy again.

All the time Grandpa must have known what was in his mind, for now he straightened up his back, looked at the rain a moment and then said: "Well, Davie, it must be getting close to noon now. And do you know what your mother told me this morning? She told me she was going to fry herring! Not only for your family, but for Grandma and me too. So I thought up a scheme while you were in there. Your mother must be frying those herring right now, and if you hurry home, I wouldn't be a bit surprised if she gave you a nice golden herring. Doesn't she usually give you the broken ones? If you eat that herring, and then hurry back here, you can have

76

lunch with us—and another herring! And if there's anything better than one herring, it's two herrings!"

"Oh, Grandpa, that's a wonderful scheme! And it's a wonderful room, Grandpa," he blurted. "But Grandpa, today. . . . Might I go in there some other day and . . ." He didn't quite know how to say it and he searched his grandfather's face anxiously.

Grandfather understood. "Sure, Davie. I know how it is today. But now you'd better run to Grandma and ask her for my umbrella, so you can go home through the rain. And just think, right after that lunch of herring, why, it'll be afternoon!"

"Yes, Grandpa, yes," he shouted. He had to dash then. Pelt through the rain, throw the house door open. He shouted all the way down the hall. "Grandma, Grandma, I've got to have Grandpa's umbrella—Grandpa said so. But I'm coming right back to have lunch with you and Grandpa." He had all his explaining done by the time he burst into the room where Grandma was. He stood before her. "And Grandma, after that it'll be afternoon!"

"So it will, so it will," Grandma said. "My, oh my, Davie, such an excitement!" She got up,

77

but then she still had to search in all kinds of corners and way back in a closet for Grandpa's umbrella. Oh, she was slow! Now at last she came backing out of the closet with the umbrella. "Well, that will be nice—you having lunch with us," she was saying. He wanted to grab the umbrella, but he knew Grandma would first want a kiss. Grandma always wanted a kiss. He kissed her. "My, Davie, one little skinny peck for all that trouble?" But she handed him the umbrella. He grabbed it and dashed.

"I'll be right back!" he shouted over his shoulder. But he came storming back. "Grandma, what time is it?"

He could tell time himself now, but he couldn't take the time to puzzle it out for himself. Grandma peered hard at the clock. "Why, it's after twelve! Five minutes after twelve. But I think that clock is five minutes fast. . . ."

"I'll be right back, Grandma!"

He tore past the wide open door of the barn. "It's twelve o'clock, Grandpa," he yelled loudly. "It's noon, and then it'll be afternoon." He did not stop or slow down.

"So it will, so it will, Davie."

Grandpa's words came out of the barn and seemed to follow him.

CHAPTER 6

He folded the dripping umbrella and set it just inside the door of the long hallway. The whole hall was delicious with fried fish odors. Mother *was* frying fish.

"Yum, herring!" he said to his mother in the kitchen, as if it were a big surprise and he hadn't known. "Mom, you know what's better than one herring? Two herrings!"

His mother smiled but she did not answer at once. She was busy turning the herring, the sputtering in the frying pan changed to a flaming sizzle, steamy wonderful odors rose up from the stove. "Two herrings, hunh?" his mother said at last. "That sounds like Grandfather. Have Grandpa and you had your heads together again, cooking up schemes?"

"He told me you were going to fry fish," he said carefully. "And I thought that maybe it might be that there'd be a broken one."

"Well, and I thought now if I fry some herring maybe it might be that I can get Davie to come home. Are you going to live in that barn? But no—no broken ones! You'd think, as fresh and fat as these were, that they'd break from sheer richness. Why, they were so fresh out of the sea, I sort of had to slap them down to keep them in the frying pan!"

He chuckled his delight. Mother could say such funny things—not often, but sometimes—and then it was such fun because it was such a surprise.

His mother dug forcefully with her spatula under the fish in the frying pan. "Well, now," she exclaimed—as if she hadn't done it on purpose—"if I didn't go and break one right then and there! But that must be from excitement at seeing you home. You've become such a stranger, it makes me a little nervous when you pay me a visit."

He was delighted. He loved her. He stood close to the stove, wordlessly admiring his mother. He tried hard to think of something to say, so she'd go on being funny. She was so nice when she was funny like that.

"Clumsy!" he said at last. It was the best he could think of, to tease her.

"Well, now, Davie!" Mother said. "Well, just for that remark, you're going to sing for your herring. No song, no herring."

He started to laugh, but just like that Mother turned serious. "Sing me a song, Davie," she pleaded. "The way you used to sing for me."

He looked up at her steadily. Now she was serious. She could make you feel so nice and chuckly, and all in a moment it would be gone and she'd be serious.

"Sing what?" he said, unwilling.

"Sing what! Davie, you know all kinds of songs. Before you were sick you used to sing just one hymn after the other. Why, even when you were very little and still in your high chair you used to sing all kinds of songs. People used to stop outside to listen—it was like a little angel singing."

He squirmed.

"You haven't forgotten them?" Mother asked

anxiously. "You didn't lose them all while you were sick so long?"

He shook his head. "No."

"Well, but you haven't sung at all again since you were sick."

"Oh, I sing all right," he said shortly. "But I sing the songs inside of me now."

"Oh, I'm glad to hear that! I was really worried. But Davie, I can't hear the songs you sing inside. That was just a joke about singing for a herring. You just sing one of those beautiful hymns for me right now."

"Which one?" he asked. Mother had spoiled it all now. It would have been fun singing for a herring. He could have made believe he was a beggar come to the kitchen for a handout, or a bum even!

"Oh, just pick the one that you like best," Mother was saying. She looked so anxious and serious that he obediently stepped away from the stove and began to sing the hymn that had sung itself inside his mind ever since he had named the little rabbit. The high notes fluted out of him as if they came from a separate little voice he kept tucked away in a separate secret little throat. Mother stood listening.

"He's the lily of the valley," his high singing

82

voice was announcing. The words came out like little bells.

"The bright and morning star." His voice went down, feeling its way among the nimble, soft, sweet words.

"He's the Fairest of Ten Thousand to My Soul!"

It burst out of him. It filled the kitchen. Inside of him it felt like a great, great, mighty shout.

He broke off. "Mom?" he said. "Is it wicked to think of my little rabbit when I sing 'fairest of ten thousand to my soul?' Mom, I sing it inside of me all the time when I think of my little rabbit coming. Is that wicked, Mom?"

She caught him up, held him hard against her soft chest. "Oh, I guess it is a little wicked, Davie. But if it is, then I'm wicked too. Because you're the fairest of ten thousand to my soul! No, if that is wicked, we'll just have to be a little wicked together, you and I. I can't help it, because when I think of how close I came to losing you when you were so sick . . ."

That was wonderful—Mother and he both

being a little wicked together. Both of them! He started to laugh. It made him feel good. But there were tears in the corners of Mother's eyes. Immediately it changed everything, it made him feel wooden and clumsy and mushy. He held himself very still, because he wanted to squirm  and wriggle free from her —but that would hurt Mother. He held himself heavy, and she had to lower him to the floor. "Now may I have my herring?" he asked quickly.

She gave him a quick kiss, and then she put the herring on a plate and put it on the table. She pulled up a chair for him. She did everything for him as if he were a helpless baby!

He fidgeted, sat kicking his legs under the table. Mother still had the tears in the corners of her eyes. He looked right at her. "Mom," he said, "I've been sick, but I'm not sick any more." He looked right at her.

"Yes, thank God," she said, and her eyes went bright with tears. He fidgeted under the table. The steamy warm smell of the herring rose up under his nose. He turned his attention to the herring. Oh, it smelled good. He pulled the hot fish apart, stuffed the biggest boneless piece steaming hot in his mouth. Oh, it tasted good. Suddenly he couldn't swallow. He couldn't swallow it!

"What is it, Davie, a bone in your throat?" His mother stooped over him anxiously.

"No, I can't swallow," he mumbled. "It's because of the little rabbit," he explained so she wouldn't stand there worrying. "I can't eat when Shadrach's coming so soon."

"Shadrach? Oh, your little rabbit. No, I suppose you can't—you're over-excited. It isn't even good to eat when you're so excited. But don't worry, I'll save you some. Then after the rabbit has come and all the excitement has died down, you can eat. I think that would be better for you."

"Yes," he agreed. He wanted to be away, but he felt guilty at wanting to leave so soon. He wished he hadn't gagged over the herring—it had smelt so good, and then all of a sudden . . . He stood there not knowing what to do.

"Why don't you visit with your father in the carpenter shop for a while," his mother said. "That'll help make the time pass until Maartens comes." She set the herring out of sight.

"All right, Mom," he agreed. "'Bye, Mom.

You'll come to the barn to see my little rabbit when it comes, won't you?"

"Oh, I surely will. I don't think I could eat either if I had a little rabbit coming. Why, I'm as excited about that rabbit as you are."

"You are? Oh, Mom!" he said. He stood there and felt clumsy and wooden. He ought to run up and kiss her, but she still had that moist look of tears in her eyes. Suddenly he turned and bolted down the hall, but all the way down the hall he sang: "He's the fairest of ten thousand to my soul." Sang it just as loud and hard as he could, for mother. He stopped to grab the umbrella. "Mother," he shouted back to the kitchen, "Grandpa gave me his big umbrella so I wouldn't get wet."

He made sure she heard it so she wouldn't worry about his getting soaked, because he had decided not to go to the carpenter shop. He was going to the dike. He had to go to the dike—he had to see if Maartens was coming!

The wind was hard and gusty on top of the dike. It came over the sea. But the heavy rain shut out the sea, except for the dirty spumy waves that lapped part way up the dike. There was nothing on the dike but grazing sheep.

86

They started to follow him, glad to see some-body in the dreary rainy day. He walked fast ahead of the sheep until he came to the iron fence that held the sheep from straying too far from the village. He peered over the fence through the mists of rain down the long narrow road that ran along the foot of the dike. Down that road Maartens had to come. But there was nothing. The road lay empty.

The sheep began to crowd in on him. The whole flock gathered around him so close that he was getting wet from their heavy soaked wool. He shoved them aside, but they kept pressing back. He had to fold the umbrella and climb to the top of the fence to get away from them. He stood balancing and teetering on the flat top rail of the fence.

The sheep bleated up at him, but he paid them no attention and stood peering. There still was nothing moving on the rainy, misty, cold road. Then, as if out of nowhere, something came looming out of the mist and rain. It looked like a horse. It was a horse and wagon! It was Maartens, it must be Maartens' old white horse. It was the canvas-covered chinaware wagon!

With a wild yell that scattered the sheep he jumped down from the fence and tore along the dike back to the village. The sheep ran bleating out before him, scattered clumsily down the dike in all directions. He ran hard, but he came to sudden scared halts, suddenly worried that it wasn't Maartens after all. Far down the dim road the old white horse came on with the looming canvas wagon behind him. Oh, it was Maartens! It was just that the wagon looked different with a canvas stretched over it. Maartens had stretched a canvas over it to keep the dishes dry, to keep the little black rabbit dry. Little black rabbit. . . . Shadrach. Shadrach.

He raced headlong down the dike steps, and started to run down the street into the village to tell Grandpa. Suddenly he turned and ran out to meet Maartens instead. He ran far down the road, but his hard run came to a sudden halt. The old horse had turned off! There went the wagon in a sharp turn into a distant side road. The wagon was going away! He stood forlorn and dismayed in the middle of the rainy road. Then he remembered that far down that side road stood three houses. Maartens must be going to stop there first before coming to the village.

He ached to follow the distant wagon. He didn't know what to do. No, he'd better tell

Grandpa. That's what he'd do—tell Grandpa Maartens was coming, Maartens was on the way!

It started to rain harder, and he put up the big umbrella and ran with it. Then he was running past his own house. The umbrella bothered him. He opened the door and threw the hastily folded umbrella into the hall. "Mom, Mom," he yelled. "Maartens is coming down the road. Maartens is coming!" He dashed on again, on to Grandpa's.

He was far down the street when his mother called from the door: "Davie, Davie, not so fast, not so hard! Davie, your umbrella!"

He made believe he did not hear, raced on.

Grandfather wasn't in the barn. He stormed into the house. Grandpa and Grandma were eating. It brought him up short, he hadn't expected that. Now he couldn't ask Grandpa to go out to Maartens' wagon with him, not when Grandpa was eating.

"Grandpa," he panted. "Maartens is coming! He'll soon be in the village, he's just stopping at those three houses out on that side road, and then he'll be here. And it's raining hard. Oh, Grandpa!"

Grandpa tried to calm him. "Look, Davie,

Maartens has to make many a stop at the outlying houses before he gets into the village, so there's plenty of time. Suppose you just sit nicely down with us to eat. Oh, that herring's good!"

"I can't eat," he said impatiently. "And Mother says I shouldn't eat when I'm so excited."

"Oh," Grandpa grunted. "Well, may I eat, Davie? There's really plenty of time."

Grandma shook her head.

He couldn't even stand the smell of the herring. He looked anxiously out of the window, although that window didn't look out on the road at all. "I'm quick going to put some fresh food in the crib for when he comes," he suddenly decided aloud. He had to do something.

"I think that's the best idea yet," Grandpa said. "We've got to have everything ready."

He dashed to the barn, but there he stood. There was plenty of fresh food in the little crib. There was nothing to do. Time stood still. It was awful.

He peered out at the pouring rain. Maartens would stop at all the outlying houses before coming into the village—stand there in the rain waiting at each house. . . . He could stand the waiting no longer. Waiting was just like pain. It hurt. He wished he hadn't thrown the umbrella in Mother's hallway. If he had the umbrella, he could go out to look for the wagon, follow it even. . . . But the way it was pouring now he knew that if he went home, Mother wouldn't let him go out again. He thought of something. Grandpa always pulled a sack over his head and shoulders when he got caught in the rain on his farm. He grabbed a sack and draped it over his head and shoulders. Then he dashed.

He ran hard all the way out of the village, all the way to the little side road. Just as he reached it, there Maartens' old horse came turning out of it. Now the wagon was coming toward him. All of a sudden there they were. He stood at the side of the road, the words all ready in his mouth to say to Maartens, "Hello, Maartens. Maartens, have you got my little rabbit?"

The wagon passed him so close, the hub of the front wheel almost grazed him. But Maartens became busy ringing a bell to announce to the village that he was coming. Maartens didn't even see him. Maartens looked cross and wet and angry, and everything dripped with rain. The words had been ready in his mouth, but all of a sudden he went shy and couldn't think of them. When he thought of them, the wagon was past.

Dumbly, miserably he started to follow the wagon. There was nobody in the streets, just the old wagon in the rain, just he behind the wagon, walking under his sack. Nobody stopped the wagon. Now and then a woman took the trouble to open the door a moment, and shout: "Nothing today, Maartens." Up at the front on the high seat he could hear Maartens muttering to himself in the rain. The old wagon lumbered on again, and he followed. Now the rain really poured down.

Then just as Maartens was beginning the
turn into a side street, a woman's voice came
through the rain, a woman was talking to Maartens. Was that Mother? The wagon had stopped,
but the rain drummed so hard on the canvas, he
couldn't be sure he had heard right. He
scrunched down, carefully peered through the
spokes of a wheel. It *was* Mother! Mother had

stopped Maartens! She had Grandpa's big umbrella. She hadn't waited for Maartens to come
to their house. . . . But what if she caught him
here in the rain, all soaked?

"Maartens, did you bring the rabbit we wrote
about?"

He had heard it plainly. Mother was shouting against the drum of the rain on the canvas.

He stood deathly still. It had never crossed
his mind—that he had never thought of—that

there might be no rabbit. He waited without a breath in his body, straining to hear what Maartens would say. The rain drummed. He hurriedly sneaked along the far side of the wagon to hear what Maartens would say.

"Now let me see, let me see," Maartens was rumbling. "Did I put that rabbit on this morning, or didn't I?"

It was unbelievable—unimaginable—Maartens' not knowing *that*!

Now Maartens was rummaging about in the wagon to see if he had brought the rabbit. It couldn't be believed!

At last Maartens spoke up. "Yup, got him. There he is all safe and snug. Tucked him so good down under the straw and stuff, I clean forgot I had him. Ho ho ho, that's a good one."

"Oh!" He felt limp.

"Thank goodness," Mother was saying. "I don't know what would have happened if there hadn't been a rabbit. It's black, I hope?"

"Black as sin," Maartens said. "You wouldn't be interested in some nice cups and saucers? Just got them in from England."

Now they were talking about dishes, not even bothering about the little rabbit. He could hold out no longer. He hurled himself around the wagon and the patient old horse. "Mother, make him give it to me," he yelled.

His mother whirled.

"Make him hand the rabbit down!"

"Davie! What are you doing here in all the rain? Look at you soaked! And that dirty, wet sack!"

He didn't care about any of it. "Make him give it to me."

"I ought to make him take it back! Look at you."

He didn't for a moment consider the threat.

Maartens was leaning down from the seat. "So, is that your boy. Why, he's been following the wagon all through the village. I was wondering what ailed the little fellow, but I never thought of the rabbit."

Now they were talking! He couldn't stand it. He tried to clamber up the spokes of the wagon to get at Maartens and the little rabbit. And now at last Maartens reached back of the seat and pulled up a little wooden box and held it down to him. There was his rabbit! He grabbed the box. It had little air holes in it. He tried to peer through one of the air holes. It was too dark. He started off with the box, turned back. "Mother, I can't see him. And it's raining, and he'll get all wet. I've got to get to Grandpa's barn. Mother!"

"Oh," she said, "so now you're worried about the rabbit getting wet!" She still had to tell Maartens a few quick last things, but then she came. She held the umbrella over him. Together they half galloped down the rainy street

under the big black umbrella. He hugged the box to his chest. "Oh, Mother."

"Yes—oh, Mother—but you're soaked and cold and chilled, and the moment you get your rabbit in that hutch, you're going straight to bed."

He knew it for the hollow threat it was, he didn't even listen to it. "Mom, Grandpa and Grandma will be sitting there eating, and all the time we'll have the little rabbit in the hutch, and then we'll tell Grandpa. You know what? We'll tell him there's some animal in the barn. A rat! And there he'll come, maybe with a club, even. And all the time it will be my little black rabbit, and then he'll see it. . . . Mom, you can't run very fast, can you? Oh, Mom, I've got my little rabbit. And Mom, you went after him too."

"Yes," Mother said. "I wanted to surprise you. I just wanted to see your face."

"Oh, Mom," he said, and it had to express all his great gratitude and all his excitement. "Mom, can't we go faster?"

At last they were there. And Mother had the top of the hutch open, and he had his hand down in the dark box, and in his hand was something silky, furry, and warm. It moved—*it lived*! Soft and warm and it lived! Gently, a little fearfully, he lowered the little black furry handful into the hutch, scared and careful not to clutch too hard, and afraid at the same time the little rabbit might wriggle free and fall to the ground and hurt himself.

There he was—there sat the little furry ball, black on the gleaming yellow straw. There he was in the hutch. Shadrach! He wanted badly to take him out again, didn't dare take him out again—no, he was safer in the hutch. But for a moment he had held him, felt him—alive!

"There he is. Mom, there he is!" But under his breath he kept saying: "Shadrach, Shadrach, little black rabbit." And all through him it sang, sang like a storm: "Fairest, fairest, fairest of ten thousand to my soul."

"Oh, he's black," Mother was saying. "Not a white hair on him. But weren't you going to run and tell Grandpa?"

At that moment the little black ball that had been sitting in the straw, moved, hopped. In two slow hops it came, and then a little wriggling nose pressed between the slats.

He was suddenly weak. He sat down flat on the ground in front of the hutch. "Mom, you tell Grandpa and Grandma," he begged hoarsely. He couldn't take his eyes off the little black rabbit. "Mom, will you?" he urged.

"Must I tell him your story about the black animal that might be a rat, and tell him to bring a club?"

He shook his head. This was no time for baby jokes like that. This, this was—holy.

CHAPTER 7

Let's see, he'd had the little rabbit two weeks now. Oh, it couldn't be! Yes, it was two weeks, because he'd been back at school a whole week now, and this was the last long afternoon of his first week back at school. The first wonderful week he'd had Shadrach, Mother had still kept him out of school. Dad hadn't liked it, but Grandfather had said it would be good for him to be out in the open. "Give him another week," Grandfather had said. "He can catch up. School's for dumb kids, isn't it? To make them smart. But if you start out smart, then you get so all-fired smart from going to school, there'll just be no keeping house with Davie."

He chuckled. Grandpa was funny. He heard himself chuckle and he quickly looked around to see if anybody in the school room had heard, but it must have been an inside chuckle, for nobody in the room seemed to have noticed. It was lucky, because Teacher had said this morning—right out before the whole class—that he didn't want to catch him dreaming in school again. But now Teacher was busy with the other class, the sun was warm on the windows, the arithmetic lesson was easy to do, and the afternoon was long and dull and endless.

To think that he'd had Shadrach two weeks now! It was almost unbelievable, and it was still a miracle. Every morning you woke up it was a miracle all over again, that there in a barn across the village sat a little rabbit, and he was yours. Something breathing, nibbling, hopping, and it was yours! In all the world it was yours. It was alive, and it was yours!

Oh, but it had been nice the way they all had come to look at Shadrach that first great day. It was even nicer because they had come one by one. First there had been Mother, of course, because she'd helped him carry Shadrach from Maartens' wagon to the barn. But Mother had gone to get Grandpa. And Grandpa had come with a plate, and on it was a fried herring. Grandpa had put two potato crates right in front of Shadrach's hutch, and Grandpa had sat there with him.

"Now while you look your fill, you go and eat

your fill of that delicious herring," Grandpa had said. "Grandma kept it warm for you."

It had been wonderful sitting there close, talking and talking about the little rabbit. All about Shadrach, the way he hopped, the way he nibbled and wriggled his little nose, about how black he was—black as sin—about his ears, his little two-cent tail—that's what Grandpa had called it—and everything and everything all over from the beginning again about Shadrach. Grandpa had kept reminding him to eat, and he'd kept forgetting because there'd always been something else again to point out to Grandpa about Shadrach. Shadrach, Shadrach, little black rabbit. . . .

Then Grandma had come, and Grandma had sat in the exact spot where Grandpa had sat. She had sat there just like Grandpa, leaning forward, peering into the hutch with her old eyes. She had even cleaned her glasses with the inside bottom edge of her apron. That had been nice, too—Grandma there—because he had been able to tell Grandma not only everything about Shadrach, but also everything that Grandpa had said about Shadrach. And Grandma had just sat there saying: "My, oh my, oh my, Davie." Finally he'd just had to put down his plate with the herring and lay his head on Grandma's knee and say: "Oh, Grandma!" He had loved her so.

Then Mother had been back again, with dry clothes. There in the barn she'd made him undress down to his skin, right before Grandma!

But she'd first put a potato sack down on the earthen floor for him to stand on. Mother had said: "I just thought I'd better bring these here, because I know you won't stir from this barn the rest of this day."

She'd rubbed him so hard with a dry towel to get the chills and dampness all out of him that he'd had to put his hands on Grandma's shoulders—otherwise Mother would have rubbed him right down to the floor. And Grandma had said: "My, oh my, oh my, Davie, to think that your grandfather thought of giving you a little rabbit! I don't think he could have thought of anything better in all the world."

Grandpa couldn't have!

Then Dad had come! There all of a sudden Dad's voice had come through the open doorway: "Is this where that eighth wonder of the world is kept? Is it in this barn? Can anybody tell me?"

He'd dragged his father over to the hutch, but Dad had been in too big a hurry to sit down on the potato crate. He'd just stood stooped over the hutch, slowly wiping the rain spots from his glasses. It had made him so impatient, he'd just yelled at Dad: "Look at him, Dad!"

Dad had said: "I'm looking and looking with my whole pair of eyes, and even an extra pair of glasses thrown over them." Dad always had such funny sayings!

But then he'd said: "Is that the little beastie, Davie? Is he black! I don't think I could have made a better black rabbit myself out of a piece of black ebony."

He'd told Dad: "Your old wooden rabbit you would make would just sit!"

"So." Dad had said. "SO! I'm good enough to make your rabbit hutches, but not your rabbits." Dad had tried to look terribly hurt but he hadn't managed at all. Oh, he loved his dad! He just had to tell Dad: "Dad, I named him after our game."

"What game?" Dad had said. He hadn't remembered!

"Our And-Abed-We-Go game, don't you remember?" he had to tell Dad. "When you used to toss me up in bed before I got sick. Dad, when are we going to start playing it again?"

"We aren't," Dad had said. "That was before you were sick so long, but now you're a big grown healthy school boy, so we can't play those little kid games any more." For once Dad had been serious.

Because Dad had been serious, he had told him something then that he'd been thinking over for a long time. And it was serious, too, and not funny! He'd told Father right out: "You want to make me big all of a sudden, but Mother wants to keep me sort of sick, and sort of a baby."

Although it was serious, and it wasn't funny.

Dad had laughed and laughed. But then he'd said: "My boy, I think you've got the rat right by the clean, naked tail there."

It was one of Dad's funny, strange sayings that he never could puzzle out the meaning to right away, so he'd had no answer. Dad had gone away—he was always in a hurry—but he *had* poked his head back around the corner of the door. "It's a wonderful little rabbit, Davie. Take good care of him. But you didn't tell me which one of the men from our to-bed-game you named him after?"

"Shadrach."

"I see," Dad had said, "the first one. I see! That leaves room in the hutch for Meshach and Abed-nego."

He didn't want any other rabbits—only Shadrach!

Rem hadn't come to see Shadrach until the following Monday. It would have been better if Rem hadn't come at all! Rem had been out in the fields, jumping ditches that whole rainy Saturday. He'd come home way late, all soaked and muddy. He'd had to go to bed without supper. Rem hadn't even been able to come to see Shadrach the next day on Sunday, because for punishment Rem had had to stay in the house all Sunday—except to go to church, of course.

That wonderful Saturday afternoon had come to an end. It had got dark, too dark to see Shadrach in the hutch even. Mother had come to take him home. "Or should I make a bed for you here in the barn?" she'd said. "So you could sleep with your Shadrach."

He wouldn't have minded! Except the barn got so dark!

Rem had come to look at Shadrach on Monday. Monday had been a beautiful sunshiny day. It was after school and when he had come into the barn, there Rem had been—the coop open and Shadrach out of the coop! Rem had been holding Shadrach up by the skin of his neck!

"Don't!" he'd yelled at Rem.

"Don't you know that's the way you're supposed to hold a rabbit?" Rem had said in his know-it-all-big-brother voice.

He hadn't believed Rem for one moment. It hadn't seemed right. It looked all wrong, for there Shadrach had hung with his hind legs cramped up just as if he had a stomach ache. There had been nothing he could do, Rem woudn't have paid any attention anyway.

Rem had said: "He's a buck. It's not a doe."

He didn't care! He'd never even given that

a thought. He'd just wanted Rem to put Shadrach back in the hutch.

"If it was a doe," Rem had said, "you could raise little rabbits. We could take Grandpa's potato crates and nail them to the wall clear up to the rafters. We'd have the whole side of the barn full of rabbits, and then we'd skin them and sell their skins."

He didn't want a whole barnful of rabbits—just Shadrach. Skin them! The thought had made him feel crawly and sick inside. It still did, even sitting here in school!

"I know how to skin rabbits," Rem had said. He didn't care if Rem did! But then Rem had said: "Look, Davie—  never hold a rabbit by the ears. Like this!" And then he'd done it! Held Shadrach up by the ears! There Shadrach had dangled and twisted, long and limp and straight, with eyes almost popping out.

He'd looked for something in the barn— quick—to hit Rem with! He hadn't seen anything quick enough, so he'd grabbed the wooden shoe off his foot, and he'd gone after Rem with that.

Rem hadn't been scared. "Well, now what's the matter with you?" Rem had said. "I was just showing you, wasn't I? Lots of kids hold rabbits that way, but it isn't good for them and then they stay skinny and won't grow at all."

If Rem hadn't put Shadrach back in the hutch right then, he'd have hit Rem.

Rem had said: "He's skinny!"

"He isn't either," he'd yelled back at Rem. Why hadn't Rem gone away? Nobody'd asked him to come!

And then the awful thing had happened. Rem had seen a piece of fishpole stuck in the beams right above Shadrach's hutch. "Hey, Davie," Rem had said, "let's go minnow fishing! Want to go minnow fishing with me? You go get a bowl from Grandma, then I'll catch you some minnows, and you can keep them in the bowl on Grandma's mantel."

He had run hard as he could to get the bowl from Grandma—just to get Rem away from the barn. But when he had come tearing back, there Rem had stood right on top of Shadrach's hutch, trying to reach the fishpole. Everything had groaned and bent, but Rem had stretched still higher. With a little jump he'd made a grab for the fishpole, but he'd lost his balance. Rem had quick stepped back, but not far enough—he'd stepped right on the little crib. *Crack*—with an awful tearing sound one end of the crib had ripped away. And there it had hung.

Then Rem had been sorry and chummy and nice, when it was too late! Rem had tried to shove the crib back around the nails, but everything was splintered and broken. But Rem had just run out and grabbed a few bricks out of the yard, and he'd propped up the hanging end of the crib with bricks. "We'll fix it all up when we get back from fishing," Rem had promised him. "We'll first quick catch some minnows before it gets dark."

"Aw, go away," he'd said inside himself, because inside of him everything had been sick and crying, only he hadn't shown it before Rem. "Aw, bawl baby!" Rem would have said. "I'm going to fix it, ain't I?"

He wouldn't even let Rem fix it! And he hadn't gone with Rem to catch minnows. Rem had promised that he'd bring him three minnows in Grandma's bowl, the biggest ones he could catch. Who had cared?

When Rem was gone he had tried in every way to fix the broken crib himself, but always the broken end had come sagging down again. At last he had just sat there, because he'd felt so hopeless. He couldn't fix anything!

Grandma had come into the barn and found him crying. It had helped to tell Grandma everything. Grandma had just said over and

over: "Oh, that Rem. That Rem! Always so rough and thoughtless." That had helped too, but it hadn't fixed the crib. Grandma had puttered with it, but she had been no good at it either, and at last she'd just said: "You come in the house with me and have a glass of milk and a cookie. I'm sure Grandpa can fix it with some wire to hold it up there nice and snug and proper."

They'd had to prop the crib back on Rem's bricks, exactly the way Rem had done it. If only there had been some other way than Rem's way —but there had seemed to be no other way.

Rem must have been really sorry though, for he *had* brought him the bowl with three big minnows in it. For a couple of days they'd stood on Grandma's mantel, but then they'd died.

The minnows had died, but the crib still stood propped up on Rem's brick's. Nobody had fixed it. Grandpa had come home very late that evening, because it was potato planting time. He had looked at the crib, but he'd just said: "Oh, that will hold all right for now, Davie. That's a job for a rainy day—the first rainy day I'll fix it up proper." Grandpa had been angry though, and he'd said something about forbidding Rem the barn. But nothing had come of that. And the crib was still propped up on Rem's bricks, and no rainy day had come, and Dad didn't have time to fix it either.

Mother had said it wouldn't be right to pester poor Dad with it. Dad was building a big complicated farmhouse, Dad had problems of his own. Dad had put him off, too. Dad had said he didn't know when he could do it, unless it was on Sunday. But that wouldn't be right—to work on Sunday! "Some rainy day, Davie," Dad had said.

Now it was almost two weeks, but it didn't rain, and didn't rain, and the minnows were long dead, and the crib was still broken. It spoiled something, just knowing that the crib was there in the barn propped up on bricks. He'd wake up in the morning knowing it the first thing, and he'd think about it even in school! Nobody seemed to care, nobody even thought about the broken crib anymore, or about Shadrach. Nobody!

They had all laughed at him because he had gathered three bags of clover for Shadrach a week too soon. Grandma had even said that day: "What's it going to be, Davie? Three sacks a week too early, and after you've had him a week the poor little animal can grunt from hunger?"

Rabbits didn't grunt! Anyway they'd been all wrong. He hadn't forgotten, they'd forgotten! They were the ones who'd forgotten Shadrach and the broken crib, he hadn't. He worried about it every day, and he fed Shadrach every day—and not just any old thing either! He knew where every tender, milky dandelion grew on the way to school. He knew every patch of sweet white clover that wasn't dusty from road dust, and he never brought Shadrach even one single stalk of tall red clover that would make

Shadrach bloat. And almost every day he went way out to Grandpa's farm to get young lettuce for Shadrach.

He wished school was out—it ought to be almost out. The moment it was out he'd go right straight from school—he wouldn't even go home first—to get some nice young lettuce from Grandpa's farm. There was milk in young lettuce, too!

The bell rang. He crammed his things into his desk and was the first one out the door.

The barn door was locked. The house door was locked. Grandma must be gone, and she'd locked the doors. There he stood with his bunch of lettuce and dandelions. Everything was shut tight. It was a woeful feeling. He couldn't get to Shadrach, he couldn't do anything—all of a sudden there was nothing to do. The yard looked so empty and quiet. He stuffed the lettuce and dandelions under an upside-down pail and went home.

Mother *was* home. She sat darning socks. "Well, you're home early!" she said surprised. "Did the teacher chase you home for sitting dreaming about Shadrach again?"

"No," he said in a lost, empty voice. "Grand-

113

ma's gone and she locked the barn door. May I have a glass of milk?" He didn't particularly want milk, but the afternoon seemed endless and empty before him, and he couldn't think of a thing to do. He sipped thin little sips out of the glass of milk just to make it some sort of a game. He looked over his glass at his mother.

"Mother," he said, "how did you happen to think of going out to Maartens' chinaware wagon that afternoon that Shadrach came?"

He waited with the milk, but Mother just eyed the sock she was darning. She shook her head over all the holes in it. "You know," he prompted, "I'd thrown Grandpa's wet umbrella in your nice clean hall."

Now Mother knew that he wanted the story of Shadrach once more. She didn't say: "Oh, Davie, you know it backward and forward, I've told you that story so often!" He was glad she

114

didn't because it would have spoiled something. He couldn't explain it to Mother, but it was with the story just like with a hymn. You knew every word and note of it, but you liked it every time again, just because you *did* know the words and the notes.

His mother was shaking her head. That was the way to begin the story! She was shaking her head over him and what he'd done the day that Shadrach came. "There I found that wet umbrella sprawling right across the middle of my nice waxed linoleum," Mother began. "Oh, it made me so impatient! There I was grumbling and wiping up that puddle and saying to myself: 'Now why did that *kid* throw it here when it's raining cats and dogs and he'll get soaked to the skin?'"

He loved that! He chuckled his delight—Mother saying *kid. That kid!* It sounded so—well, it almost sounded like Mother was swearing, because she never said kid, only in the story. And it always made him feel sort of rough and dirty and with his nose unwiped when Mother said *that kid* about him. Just as if he were a stranger—one of those strange dirty kids that came to the village on the canal boats. Why, it was almost as if Mother didn't know him, and he didn't know Mother. "That kid!" he said delightedly, and sipped a little milk.

Mother made believe she hadn't heard him. "And there I was wiping away at that puddle," she said again, "and suddenly it popped into my mind: Why don't I surprise him? Why don't I surprise Davie right out of his skin? Why don't I take the umbrella and go out and meet Maartens' wagon, and then I'll secretly bring the little rabbit to the barn and put him in his hutch. There Davie will be sitting at Grandpa's eating herring, and I'll walk in just as innocent and empty handed and say: 'Oh, there you are, Davie! Suppose when you've finished with your herring, you and I go out to fetch that rabbit from Maartens?' "

And then after a little pause Mother added: "As if you could have eaten even one single crumb of herring after that!"

Oh, he was glad Mother had added that this time. The last time she'd told the story, she'd forgotten.

"Oh, and in my mind I could just see what would happen," Mother was telling. "You'd jump up, herring or no herring, and you'd run out with me. But we'd have to go past the barn, and then I would say: 'Hey! Maybe we'd better

116

have a look at that hutch first to see if everything is shipshape.'

"And in my mind I just knew what would have happened then. You'd have practically yelled at me: 'Of course, Mother, everything's shipshape!' And you wouldn't have wanted to go in the barn with me, you would have been so impatient to get to Maartens' wagon. But I would have gone in just the same, and you would have been standing there in the doorway, so impatient with me you'd have wanted to wring my neck!"

That was good! That was new. Mother hadn't ever put that in the story before. Imagine him wanting to do that—why he'd never even thought of such a thing in all his life. He shoved the glass of milk aside, he leaned on the table. "And then, Mom," he urged.

Mother pretended to be studying the darn she had just finished in the sock, just to keep him waiting. "And then," she said slowly, but she still had to turn the sock around once more. "And then—then I would have made believe I was looking inside the hutch, and I would have called out to you: 'But, Davie, I thought you'd put clean straw in here—what's this straw doing so black?'

"Then you'd have come running all right —and there would sit your little *Shadrach*!" Mother looked at him. "End of the story," she said.

Mother always said that at the end. He laid his chin on his arms on the table and looked up at her and sighed. "Oh, Mother, that would have been wonderful! But it wouldn't have been quite so wonderful as the way it really happened, would it?"

"No, I was a little bit disappointed that you'd spoiled my big secret surprise—there I sneaked to Maartens' wagon, and who should be there behind that wagon but you with a sack thrown over your head, for all the world like a mourner at a funeral. And *soaked*! There went my whole big secret plan. But I've got to admit it just couldn't have been so wonderful as the way it really happened."

That is what he had wanted to hear. He pushed his chair back. Now he had to dash off to see Shadrach. "Will Grandma be home now?" he demanded. He had to go see Shadrach! He didn't know why, but always that story of Mother's made everything seem right and good again—even the broken crib. He sighed deeply. One little thing still nagged at the back of his mind. He had to tell Mother, now.

118

"Mother, the first day everybody came to look at Shadrach, but now nobody ever looks at him any more. And nobody has time to fix the crib."

"Don't you believe it!" Mother said. "I want you to know that every afternoon when I go to Grandma's for a cup of tea, I stop in the barn to look at your Shadrach—even before I go in the house."

"Every day?" he asked. He stood amazed.

"Every day!" Mother said.

Everything eased in him. He stood there marvelling at his lovely mother.

"Don't you think that I don't!" Mother said stoutly. "And don't you think that I'm going to let them forget that broken crib. It's going to be fixed—the minute there's a minute."

"The minute there's a minute," he repeated softly. Then he had to dash, gallop loud and hard down the long hall. Sing it out—the minute there's a minute. Why, it was a song! It was a ready made inside song, from Mother. "The minute there's a minute. The minute there's a minute."

He tried it out again on the street. He jumped and danced and skipped to it. He danced back a few steps. "The minute there's a minute!"

He saw a tiny toy fence around some gera-

119

niums in a little front yard. He jumped over the little fence, flowers and all. A woman rapped sharply on the window, she stayed there looking very sour-faced through the pane. He was terribly tempted to do it again—jump it both ways, flowers and all, in spite of the sour-faced woman. But he dashed off to the barn to see Shadrach.

Oh, Mother hadn't forgotten Shadrach. Every afternoon she looked at him. She couldn't fix the crib, but she would see to it that the crib was fixed. The minute there was a minute. Oh, boy! Oh man, oh man, oh man!

CHAPTER 8

Now he'd had Shadrach three weeks. But now it wasn't so wonderful any more. Oh it was still wonderful, but it wasn't wonderful with an inside singing wonderfulness. Now he didn't wake up mornings with a song already singing in him. Now he woke up worried, worried and secretly ashamed.

The broken crib was still broken, but that wasn't it. That didn't even seem so bad now. It was Shadrach, Shadrach himself. Rem had said he was skinny, and he *was* skinny! And getting skinnier, in spite of all the dandelions and lettuce and clover that he fed Shadrach. And he'd never fed Shadrach even one single stalk of tall red clover, he'd never picked up Shadrach by the ears!

"He's so skinny, all he is is just some fluffed up fur and bones—that's all," he said aloud in the room.

There now he'd said it to himself, the first thing in the morning. But now that he'd admitted Shadrach's real skinniness to himself, it worried him so that he couldn't even seem to put his stockings on. There stood the big shamed secret. Both his stockings still lay frumpled on the floor. He stared at them.

"I'm sure the answer isn't in your empty socks," Mother suddenly said. She startled him. He hadn't heard her coming. He grabbed for the stockings.

"Not those!" Mother said. "Good socks— this is Sunday."

"Oh," he said, flustered. Then he blurted it out to his mother. "Mother, Shadrach won't grow! Rem said he was skinny and he *is* skinny, and he gets skinnier every day."

"Is that what you've been brooding about these last days?"

He nodded helplessly.

"Well, now you can understand why I worry so about you when you won't eat and grow big and strong."

"But Shadrach eats!" he said impatiently.

Mother didn't have to worry about *him*! He was all right. This with Shadrach was altogether different.

"Yes, but I feel about you the same way you feel about Shadrach," Mother was saying.

He wished his mother wouldn't go on about it. His throat hurt with a dull ache. "He's all thin legs," he said bitterly. "And he's as narrow as a board when you squeeze his sides together."

"Well, maybe his bones are growing first," Mother guessed. "Some babies are that way, too —thin and long at first, but then they start to fill out. You wouldn't think now your big brother, Rem—but he was that way as a baby, thin and long and skinny."

"Rem?" he burbled. It suddenly delighted him. He sputtered and choked and laughed. "Why? Did you pick up Rem by the ears when he was a baby?"

"Well now, Davie!" His mother was scandalized. "What goes on in that mind of yours? Who ever picks up a baby by the ears!"

"Well, I don't Shadrach either, but Rem says they won't grow if you pick them up by the ears, and they'll stay skinny, but I don't."

"Well then, if you don't do it . . ."

"But Rem will say I do! He'll say that's why Shadrach stays so skinny."

"Oh, you worry too much about Rem! I'm sure Shadrach will fill out after he gets his length, and then he'll be a nice fat glossy rabbit. Why, we can even have him for a Sunday dinner."

He stared up at his mother from the floor. It was wonderful how grown-ups always had quick, easy answers ready for everything. He wasn't assured. And Mother shouldn't have joked about having Shadrach for dinner. He thought fast. Maybe now that he'd got it out and had told Mother, maybe now she'd let him. . . . "Mother, may I just run to the barn quick a minute and see if Shadrach is all right?"

"It's Sunday, Davie. And with your good clothes in that barn. . . . There isn't time. You're going to church with Dad this morning, just you and Dad out to the church in Nes. I thought that would be a big surprise treat for you, walking way out to the village of Nes with Dad. He wants to hear the new preacher there."

"Oh, good!" It was a fine surprise, but he didn't let himself forget Shadrach. "Mom, I'll just go look, I won't touch a thing, and I'll come running right back."

"Well," Mother said doubtfully. "All right, then. Otherwise I'm sure you'll just sit worrying about Shadrach all morning in church, and it doesn't seem quite right to sit worrying about a rabbit in church. But be right back!"

In the kitchen there was a bun with spice cheese on his plate on the table. He snatched it and ran hard across the village to the barn.

Shadrach was gone! The hutch was empty! Shadrach wasn't in his hutch. He stood there in his horrible scare, the forgotten bun squeezing to pieces in his hand. He stared at dim corners of the dark cluttered barn. There was nothing. Nothing moved. The whole barn felt empty. It was frighteningly quiet. He peered at the hutch in the dimness, poked at it, his face close. There was nothing. The cover of the hutch wasn't open—the brick was still on it. There wasn't any hole, not a single one of the slats was loose, nothing was disturbed, but Shadrach was gone.

He crouched at the hutch, frightened and forlorn. In the total Sunday silence of the barn and the village it seemed as if he could hear his own heart thump. He stared at the cluttered dim corners again, but there were so many nooks and holes, he didn't know where to look. He felt utterly helpless, and inside he began crying, but he did not cry out loud. The quiet was too awful to cry in. Now across the village the bell on the church tower started its solemn deep Sunday tones. Faintly far away the bell of the village of Nes began answering it. The two bells talked solemnly back and forth. It was church time.

The two bells went on ringing, there wasn't another sound. There hadn't been any sound in the barn, not a sound, but all of a sudden—there was Shadrach! There he came slowly hopping across the empty middle of the barn. Straight toward the hutch. Davie did not dare move for fear of scaring Shadrach. He crouched there, squeezing the bun. Shadrach came right to him, he even stood up against his knee like a squirrel. Why, Shadrach wanted to sniff the bun! Then he had the little rabbit, he pulled him up in his arms, he hugged him. "Oh, Shadrach, you came. You came. You came," he said brokenly. "Aw, did you want the bun?" He held the bun to Shadrach's mouth, and a Shadrach started nibbling it. Shadrach liked buns!

There were quick hard footsteps in the barn. It was Father. "What's this?" his father demanded sternly. "Didn't you promise you'd come right back?"

"Dad," he said, "Shadrach was out. Shadrach was gone and I couldn't find him anywhere. And I don't know how he got out. He just came back, just now."

"Nonsense!" his father said, not believing it for a moment. "You're just making up that story because you started playing with your rabbit and forgot to come back. Now put him in the hutch. We're late, because I was sitting home waiting for you."

Silently he dropped Shadrach in the hutch. He hurriedly glanced up, and when he saw his father wasn't looking, he dropped his bun in the hutch with Shadrach.

Straight from the barn they set out for the church in the village of Nes. He was glad they hadn't gone home first. His clean starched blouse was all smudged, there was even a black cobweb on the sleeve. He couldn't brush it off, because Dad had him by the hand. Dad didn't notice the blouse. Dad didn't notice anything, he just walked fast, staring straight ahead, not saying a word. His father walked so fast it had him running at a dog trot to keep up, but Dad still kept tugging him along.

He looked up at his staring father. Dad was still angry. He trotted on the best he could so his father wouldn't notice him. It wasn't a nice surprise trip at all. It was a headlong run without a word between him and his dad. His father seemed to be thinking hard. Well, he was thinking hard too—about Shadrach's getting out—even though it was hard to run and think at the same time. It was a mystery how Shadrach could have got out, but not a nice mystery like the ones you made up in your mind. Suppose Shadrach got out again and got lost, what then?

Words formed on the end of his tongue, but he swallowed them. Dad hadn't believed Shadrach had been out. His father thought he had fibbed. It gave him a lost, unwanted feeling. He didn't remember his father ever being really angry with him before. Oh now and then short stern words, but not really angry, not a long going-on anger like this.

All of a sudden his side started to ache and stab. It felt like a thick pincushion full of stabbing sharp pins. It felt so thick, he couldn't breathe. He still tried to trot along.

"Dad," he had to whisper at last. "Dad!" He tried to loosen his hand from his father's grasp. His father didn't even notice. "Dad! I can't any more!" He wept aloud, angrily and ashamed.

His father stopped, startled. "My side," he explained to his father between gasps. "I can't catch my breath."

"Oh Davie, why didn't you yell? Son, I forgot all about you." His father sounded sorry, his father wasn't angry!

"Here sit down quick in the grass. Sideache, hunh? Why didn't you yell, Son?"

"I thought you were angry with me." It was hard to talk between gasps, but he had to get it out now, all of it. "Dad, I wasn't fibbing—honest! Shadrach was out! I didn't let him out. And Dad, nothing was open or broken, but he was out."

He still couldn't talk right because his side was still stabbing, but he wanted to talk and talk. It was so enormously wonderful—his dad wasn't angry with him!

His father sat down in the grass beside him. "Just take deep breaths and don't try to talk. No, Davie, I wasn't angry with you. In fact, I'd

forgotten all about it. Why boy, I'd even forgotten you were with me, or I never would have
walked so fast. But I was thinking hard about
that big farmhouse I'm building. I was worrying out some of the problems in my mind."

"I was too, Dad," he said eagerly. "I was
worrying out problems about Shadrach. I was
worrying it out in my mind how Shadrach could
have got out." He laughed a little chummy
laugh and shifted closer to his father. To think
they'd both been worrying out problems!

"Tell me about it, Davie."

Now the ache was all gone. It was wonderful sitting there in the deep grass with just his father on this quiet Sunday morning. There was peace in the fields, and the whole road stretched peaceful and empty.... But they'd be late for church!

He forgot about church the next moment, for now he was telling his father everything, everything. About Shadrach's skinniness and about what Rem had said. Though he'd never picked up Shadrach by the ears and never fed him even one single stalk of tall red clover, still Shadrach stayed skinny. And now he had got so skinny, he could even get out between those narrow up-and-down slats—because that's how he must have got out. He must have squeezed out between the slats, there was no other way. He even told his father his real deep worry—something he hadn't yet dared admit to himself. There were rats in the barn—big rats, big rat holes. If Shadrach got out again, could the rats take him down one of those holes and eat him?

Off and on he almost cried a little as he talked, but that wasn't because of his worries. That was because Dad listened so seriously. Then he was finished with all he had to say, but his father didn't have a quick grown-up's answer ready for him the moment he was finished. He didn't make a joke. He sat and thought! He thought about it!

"Well, Davie," Father said at last, "I've got to admit I don't know much about rabbits. I don't know why little rabbits get skinnier and skinnier. All I know is that your mother and grandfather tell me that you take the most wonderful care of your Shadrach. Why don't you ask Grandpa—he might know. . . . So I can't do much about your rabbit, but maybe I can do something about that coop so he can't get out again. However, even though he's as skinny as you say he is, I still can't see how a rabbit could squeeze through the narrow spaces between those slats. . . . Are you sure there wasn't a loose slat, or maybe Shadrach gnawed a hole in the bottom under the straw where you didn't see it—rabbits can gnaw through wood, you know."

"I looked the hutch all over, Dad, but there were no holes, and there was nothing broken except the crib that Rem broke, but that's because you've never fixed it."

His father smiled a little at that, then he thought about the hutch again. "You're worried sick about all this, aren't you, Son?" he said. He pulled out his watch, looked at it and made a surprised sound, then pushed his watch back in his pocket. "Davie, it's much too late to go on to church now. And I've a notion that even if you and I went on to church, that preacher could preach and preach, but I'd be in that farmhouse I'm building, and you'd be in your rabbit hutch with your little rabbit. So, what do you say we go back and look at that hutch of yours?"

Oh, that was clever—the preacher could preach and preach. Why, that could be an inside song:

The preacher could preach and preach,
But you'd be in that rabbit hutch
With your little rabbit.

He loved it. He tucked it away for an inside song to remember and jumped up, eagerly ready to go back to the barn.

"We'll go back and see what we can find wrong," Dad said as they walked along. "We'll just be a little wicked today, you and I. But don't you tell anybody, not even that Grandpa of yours!"

Now it was different. Now that they were going back, he was walking eagerly ahead, almost tugging his father along. And his side didn't ache one bit. Oh, he had a wonderful father.

"Dad," he said, suddenly struck by the thought, "that's what Mom and I were once, too—a little wicked together." He told his father about "the fairest of ten thousand to my soul," and what Mother had said. "But now we're being really wicked, you and I, skipping church and going to the barn instead, and that preacher can just preach and preach. . . ."

"Well, yes, I guess so," his father said. "But you needn't feel so good about it!" Then Dad laughed, and together they hurried back to the barn.

Shadrach was still in the hutch.

His father and he were in the dark barn, and it was darker than ever, because Dad had almost pulled the big door completely shut. Oh, it was a secret as deep as a cave! Nobody could see or hear them. Grandpa and Grandma and Mother and Rem were sitting in church in the village right this minute. But he and Dad were in the barn! It seemed so secret that he even whispered to his father, and his father whispered back. Dad was feeling all around the hutch. Now he picked it up and carried it to the door so he could examine the bottom by the light from the slit of the door. And all the time Shadrach sat inside just as quiet, but the bun was gone! Shadrach had eaten the bun, he'd even eaten the spice cheese! What a queer rabbit!

"You were right, Davie," Father was saying softly. "There's nothing wrong with the hutch. And you say the cover was closed?"

"I even had a brick on it, Dad," he whispered back.

Then Dad took Shadrach out of the hutch. He held him up to the slit of light. "He *is* skinny," Dad said, puzzled. He felt Shadrach's ribs. "He isn't much wider than a board, but I can't see how he can squeeze through one of those narrow spaces between the slats. Still . . . they say a cat can get through anything just so he can get his head through. Maybe it's the same way with rabbits. Well, I can't fix your rabbit, but I think I can fix those slats."

"The crib too, Dad," he whispered urgently.

"And the crib, too," Dad said. "Even if it is Sunday, let's not forget that crib!"

Quietly they opened the door a little wider for more light so Father could hunt some slats, an old hammer, and some rusty little nails. And there on Sunday Father started nailing slats crosswise over the old up-and-down slats. The crisscross slats running across the up-and-down slats made little square holes going half way up

135

the front of the coop. It looked like a trellis. Dad had taken out his Sunday handkerchief and wrapped it over his hammer so that the hammering made soft, dull sounds—because it was Sunday. The hammer sounded muffled through the barn.

But there weren't enough slats. The crisscross slats went only half way up the front of the hutch, then there weren't any more. He and Dad searched through the whole barn, but they couldn't find another one. Then Dad fixed the broken crib—even if it was Sunday!

"There," Dad said, "now I can't see how he can possibly get out, unless he can climb like a squirrel and get above those crisscross slats."

There sat Shadrach behind the crisscross lattice work going half way up the front of his hutch. And the crib looked straight and sound and true again. It looked perfect. Shadrach pushed an inquisitive nose through one of the little square holes. He was nosy about his new coop! When Shadrach did that, he just *had* to feed Shadrach out of the new, fixed crib. He filled the crib heaping full with the freshest moist greens from the bottom of the basketful he had gathered yesterday.

Shadrach pulled a lettuce leaf through one

of the little square holes. He nibbled it inside his hutch, it made crisp sounds in the silent barn. He and Dad stood looking at Shadrach nibbling the lettuce leaf. Suddenly everything was wonderful and easy. His father had made everything seem safe and hopeful and good again. All his worries were gone. Everything was right again. It rushed through him, the grateful inside song: *Shadrach. Shadrach. Little black rabbit. Fairest, fairest, fairest of ten thousand to my soul!*

He really wanted to sing it out loud for his father, sing it loud and strong. But it was Sunday, and they were in the barn. "Oh, Dad," he whispered, and he wished his father wasn't standing up so he could lay his head against him. "Oh, Dad."

But Shadrach nibbled lettuce in the hutch, and all around lay Sunday peace, in the whole village and in the barn. And he and Father went out to walk on the dike in the quiet Sunday peace. A bell in a faraway unknown village was pealing Sunday peace. He walked very close to his father, and peace lay on the quiet sea. And the sheep followed them.

CHAPTER 9

Now he'd really have to take his secret problem to his Grandfather! Oh, not that it was really a secret any more. Mother knew about Shadrach's skinniness, and Father did. But telling Grandpa about Shadrach and his skinniness was different. Grandpa knew about animals.

Mother knew nothing about rabbits, she only seemed to know about babies. And Dad didn't know much of anything about rabbits either—he'd said so! He'd said rabbits couldn't climb—and maybe most rabbits couldn't climb, but Shadrach could! He climbed up the crisscross slats to where there were no more, then he

138

squeezed out through one of the narrow spaces between the up-and-down slats, and then he was free in the barn.

He'd seen him do it! It was easy for Shadrach. It had just so happened that he'd gone to the barn on his way back to school after his noon-hour lunch, and there was Shadrach, squeezed halfway out of the hutch. Half in, half out, with his back feet still resting on the top crisscross slat. He'd kept himself very quiet to see what Shadrach would do. Well, Shadrach had let himself drop and then he was free in the barn.

For the first time he'd been impatient with Shadrach. He'd scooped him up and shoved him back in the hutch. Shadrach had landed on his back, but he hadn't even cared—it had seemed such a shame for Shadrach to do it, after Dad had gone to such trouble to put all the crisscross slats on the hutch on Sunday. They didn't help a bit!

He still hesitated to tell Grandpa about Shadrach's real skinniness. Grandpa knew about animals. And while he knew that it wasn't his fault that Shadrach was so skinny, still somehow in some way it made him feel ashamed—a deep secret shame. He'd be late for school, too. And Grandpa would be taking his after-lunch nap.

He wasn't supposed to disturb Grandpa then, but he had to tell Grandpa—now. He didn't care, he had to! He'd be late for school—he didn't care.

He opened the door to the room very quietly. Grandpa *was* sleeping. He was in the reed chair

with a big blue handkerchief over his face against the flies. If only Grandpa had been awake. He stood very still beside the sleeping old man. Then instead of gently waking Grandfather up, he had to start to cry! That woke Grandpa up all right. He burst out with it: "Grandpa, I never pick up Shadrach by his ears,

I never have, but he just gets skinnier and skinnier, and he's so skinny he gets out between the slats, and he . . . he climbs like a squirrel. . . ."

Grandpa fumbled the handkerchief off his face and sat up. To his infinite relief he saw that Grandfather wasn't a bit impatient with him even now.

"Well," Grandpa said in a slow, half-awake voice, "if it's that bad we'd better have a look right away. But Davie, if it's that bad, why didn't you tell me before?"

"I was going to, Grandpa," he wailed. "But it made me so ashamed."

Now Grandpa started for the barn. Hopefully he trotted on behind.

Grandfather at once noticed the crisscross slats. "Who did that?"

It all came out how Dad and he had fixed the hutch last Sunday—hammered and nailed on Sunday! Because Dad had said the preacher could preach and preach, but if he, Dad, was in the farm house, and he, Davie, was in his rabbit hutch . . . It all came out very twisted, and he talked too fast because it worried him, giving away Dad's secret. "Oh, I don't care that you know, Grandpa, but I promised Dad . . ." He stopped in confusion. It didn't seem right to

141

make an old man like Grandfather promise to keep a secret.

To his amazement Grandfather started to laugh. Stood there and laughed! And Grandpa promised to keep it a secret—even without his asking Grandpa! Grandpa seemed all chuckly and pleased, and he didn't seem to mind a bit losing his after-lunch nap. Oh, he had a wonderful Grandpa.

It was easier then to open the hutch and take Shadrach out and show him in all his miserable skinniness.

Grandpa took Shadrach out of the barn into the full sunlight in the yard. He looked him all over and felt him all over; he even made Shadrach hop across the yard after giving him a little push to get him started. Shadrach hopped very slowly on his long skinny hind legs. He looked blind and bewildered and slow—he wasn't used to the sun. In a few steps Grandpa had him back again.

"Well, I don't know, Davie. There's no denying he's awfully skinny, and that isn't right, because I know you take the best of care of him and feed him only the best. It reminds me of a pig I once raised. I fed *him* only the best, and because he got only the best he became the finickiest pig. Soon he wanted nothing but the best—nothing else would do. But did he grow? He did not! He only got skinnier and skinnier. He got to be just skin and bones, and if there's anything homely it's a skinny pig. Why, he was so skinny you could almost see the sunlight though him!"

"Shadrach's all skin and bones, too, Grandpa," he said softly, "and if he didn't have black fur you could maybe see the sunlight through Shadrach." It was a miserable thing to say about Shadrach, but it was true!

"Yes, but do you know what I did to cure that pig and get him to eat and grow fat?" Grandpa said. "I got another pig. Then he started to eat —only because he didn't want the new pig to get it. He didn't want it himself, but he wanted even less for the new pig to have it, so he ate against the other pig and tried to outeat him, and then he got fat. You see, Davie, sometimes I think animals get lonely, cooped up all alone."

"But I don't have another rabbit to put in with Shadrach, Grandpa." He thought about it a little. "And . . . and I don't think I'd like another rabbit—just Shadrach." No, he was sure he wouldn't like another rabbit.

"No, but Davie, I've been thinking that

maybe you've been treating Shadrach too well, the way I did with that pig. Maybe you'll have to get a little bit rough with him—not feed him all the time and all he wants and only the things he likes. Let's take the food away from him for a day or so."

Grandpa walked to the hutch and set Shadrach in it. Then he pulled everything out of the crib.

It looked awful, the bare crib. Shadrach poked his hungry nose through one square hole after the other, but the crib was empty; it was just a bare, slanting board.

"But Grandpa, every time I go to feed him, the crib is empty," he said woefully.

"Sure, he must pull it all inside his hutch, but does he eat it? I'll bet when you clean his coop you find most of the greens all withered and trampled down in the straw, don't you?"

He had to admit it. He had to admit that these last weeks he had taken to emptying the hutch twice a week, because otherwise the straw and stuff rose so high that Shadrach almost scraped his head against the ceiling of the little hutch.

Right then and there he and Grandpa emptied the coop, and the straw was mostly withered and dried-up grass and things! Grandpa put in only clean straw, nothing else, and then he set Shadrach back on the new straw. There sat Shadrach, and he looked hungry.

It was awful leaving Shadrach behind that way, going off to school that way. But Grandpa said it was worth a try for a week. Just feed him once a day and when that's gone absolutely not a single dandelion more. One thing was sure, Grandpa said. Shadrach couldn't get any skinnier. It was true!

He walked to school very slowly, even though he was late. Now that he was on his way it worried him that he was going to be late, but he couldn't seem to hurry. He had a draggy feeling in his legs, and his stomach felt hollow and queer even though he'd just had lunch. It must be he felt that way because he thought Shadrach must feel that way, all hollow and hungry inside.

At last he got to the school. He was very late, and because he was late and had no good excuse —you couldn't tell Teacher you were late because Shadrach was so skinny—he had to stay after school. That made the long miserable afternoon all the longer. He couldn't keep his mind on anything, and nothing mattered in school.

Luckily, Teacher didn't keep him very long.

Then he tore out of school and ran hard down the road toward the barn to see how Shadrach had managed in his empty coop. He stopped short in his hard run when he saw a big dandelion rising up crisp and tasty from a ditchside. But he remembered he wasn't to feed Shadrach and he walked solemnly on, his hands feeling awfully big and empty hanging there by his sides. It was an even emptier, wretched feeling to stand empty handed before Shadrach's hutch. Shadrach looked so hungry! He poked his nose through all the square holes, but there was nothing in the empty crib.

He couldn't stand it! He knew where there was a dandelion growing behind Grandpa's compost pile. He raced out to get it. Shadrach greedily pulled the whole dandelion into his hutch in one jerk, he was that hungry!

He dashed out to find another dandelion for Shadrach. It was cheating, but he could not seem to help himself. Grandpa had said to feed him once a day, and then not a single dandelion more, and this was cheating! Suddenly he turned and tiptoed back to the hutch. Very quietly he opened the cover and watched Shadrach from up above. There lay the dandelion. Shadrach was sitting right on it. But just the same Shadrach was poking his nose hungrily through the holes, because Shadrach saw his legs standing there in front of the hutch—he didn't know he was being watched from up above. Shadrach was cheating, too! It was just as Grandpa had said. Shadrach pulled the dandelions inside his hutch, but after he had them, he didn't bother to eat them. He sat on them!

With a heavy heart he reached in, took out the dandelion, and walked away from Shadrach. In the big doorway of the barn he stared forlornly across the empty yard. He glanced hopefully toward Grandma's window, but Grandma wasn't in the reed chair. She must not be home. He couldn't go to talk to her. The whole long after-school afternoon seemed to loom empty and endless before him. There was nothing to do. It was, he suddenly thought to himself, as if Shadrach was dead.

The thought gave him such a woeful lonely feeling that he was actually glad when he heard Rem come whistling down the street. That was Rem, he knew Rem's whistle. Rem could whistle really loud and fine! Rem came into the yard, whistling away. He had a covered dish, he must be bringing something to Grandmother from

Mother. He hastily moved away from the barn door to meet Rem, otherwise Rem might want to look at Shadrach.

"Hi, Rem," he said loudly. "What you doing?"

Rem saw the limp dandelion in his hand. "How's Shadrach?" he asked.

"Oh, fine!" he said fast. "What you going to do, Rem? Can I go with you? . . . Let's go minnow fishing," he hastily thought up.

Rem just laughed about it. "No, me and the gang are going out to jump ditches—just the big draught ditches, the biggest ones we can find—and you're too small for that. You'd jump right smack in and drown! Anyway, you need a vaulting pole for jumping ditches, and you haven't even got a pole."

Just like that the thought hit him! "But I know where there is a pole I could use!" he said eagerly. "Rem, did you know that there's a big secret room right behind Grandpa's barn? It used to be Grandpa's old school, and the door to it is right in the barn, and there's all kinds of poles in there. Great big ones! The kind they push boats with down the canals, and they've got big knobs on them, even!"

Rem wouldn't believe it. Rem had never

even known about the secret room right behind the barn—and *he* had! It made him feel almost as old and big as Rem. "I was in it," he told Rem. "There's all kinds of stuff in there from ships and things and everything. Even a whole rudder! Man, you ought to see it!" Rem acted as if he didn't believe it, but he set the covered dish down on the ground right in the middle of the yard. "Where?" Rem said. "Where is that door, then?"

Rem didn't even think of Shadrach when he walked by the hutch, he was that curious. "There," he told Rem. "That's where it is, right behind those potato crates."

Rem first looked behind the crates before he would believe it, but then he swarmed right up the stack of crates. They teetered and tottered but Rem didn't care. He somehow balanced himself, and he managed to wrestle the top ones off the high pile. He just pulled them away and dropped them any place they wanted to land. After he had the top ones down, he jumped down and pushed the whole pile over. But it took all the strength Rem had to wrench the tight door open!

Together they went into the dim, dusty, boarded-up room.

"Look," he pointed out to Rem, "that's the ship's rudder. Let's climb way to the top and make believe we're sailing the sea. Look, there's the handle way up against the ceiling, we can turn it and make believe we're steering a big ship. . . ."

Rem was almost going to do it. He even started to climb up the rudder, but then he let himself drop. "Nah," he said, "that's little kid games—making believe!" Instead he stood looking around for the poles, and then he saw them in the corner. He grabbed the biggest one. "Oh, boy," he said. "What a pole for vaulting ditches!" He had to try it. He came with a run. "Stand still, Davie!" he yelled, and then he came sailing. Rem landed hard, but he picked himself up, all excited. "Oh, boy, I bet I could almost jump over a canal with a pole like this—

a side canal, anyway." He grabbed the pole. He raced toward the door.

"Can I go, too?" Davie yammered after Rem. "Rem, I want to go, too!"

Rem stopped outside the door. "No, Davie, these poles are too big for you to handle." Rem took the trouble to come back with the pole. "Just try to put your hand around it. . . . See? It's too thick. Why, you'd have all you could do to lift it!" Then Rem took the pole and ran and left him standing there alone.

He stood alone in the dim quiet room, feeling lost and cheated and left out. He stubbornly didn't cry. He felt too guilty. He'd told Rem Grandfather's big secret! Grandpa had shown him the secret room only because Grandpa had felt sorry for him, and now he'd just told Rem. Now Rem knew, and he'd come back and take things and wreck things. He'd even taken the pole! He didn't feel big now, and as if he were Rem's buddy. He felt little and cheated, deserted in the dark dusty silent room. He bolted for the door.

Out in the barn he got a terrific jolt and scare. There lay the scattered potato crates! What if Grandpa should come? Desperately he tried to shove the secret door shut. It wouldn't shut! It stuck near the top where he couldn't reach it, but the bottom gaped wide open. No matter how hard he pushed, the moment he let go, the door would spring open again at the bottom. It gaped open so wide at the bottom, he could easily push his head through! There it stuck, it wouldn't yield another inch.

He was wretchedly standing looking at the sprung door, but then he jumped. There were footsteps outside in the street, going along the barn. He could hear every one, big wooden shoes. The footsteps clattered on beyond the barn and down the street. Thank goodness, it wasn't Grandpa! But now he was more desperate than ever. He'd have to leave the door the way it was, he'd have to pile the crates in front of it so as to hide the gap at the bottom. Pile up the crates—but how?

He was scared and desperate enough to think of a way. After he had struggled the first crates into place, he found other boxes to use as steps to carry the potato crates to the top of the high stack. It was hard, sweaty, dirty work. He struggled and wrestled. Finally the last crate was on top of the high pile, but then he still had to drag the boxes he had used as steps back to their exact places all over the barn.

It was wonderful tired relief when at last he was finished. No one had come. He stepped back to study the stack of crates. It looked all right—as good as ever, almost. It hid the whole door. Nobody would ever know that the door wasn't tightly shut the way it had been before. It was all done.

Deep inside in a secret way he felt proud of himself. It had been a huge job, but he had managed all alone, nobody had helped, and nobody would ever know. He'd watch, he quickly decided, where Rem put the canal boat pole tonight, and he'd secretly bring it back to the room. Maybe he could shove it right through the opening at the bottom of the sprung door, maybe he wouldn't even have to move all the crates.

But now he'd better get out of the barn. Grandpa should be coming home any minute. He hurried out without taking time to look at Shadrach. In the yard he had another scare—there still stood the covered dish! Rem had forgotten! Rem had just run off with the pole. He glanced up the street. Grandpa wasn't coming. He looked at the window, but did not see Grandma—she still must not be home. But now around the corner and down the street there

153

came Grandpa! He grabbed up the dish and raced to the house. The door wasn't locked, but there was nobody in the house. He shoved the dish onto the edge of the table, hastily pushed it a little farther for safety, and dashed out of the house again.

Grandpa was almost to the yard now, but he couldn't face him! "Grandpa," he yelled up the street just as loud as he could, "I put a dish in the house for you and Grandma—from Mother." Then he ran.

"What's the hurry and the rush?" Grandpa called after him.

He didn't stop until he was a safe little distance down the street. "Oh," he thought up, hurriedly, "I didn't feed Shadrach, and I left the crib empty like you said, and . . ." He let his voice trail away.

"Oh, and now you can't stand to see it, so you go past the barn on a run?" Grandpa guessed.

It wasn't entirely true, but he nodded and nodded his head. Grandpa grinned understandingly, and went on into the yard.

With both his hands deep in his pockets he sauntered down the street. He shoved his hands still deeper, he felt so full of immense relief. He had done everything wrong, but everything had turned out right. Everything had gone off so fine, so fine, it could hardly be believed! Right after school the whole afternoon had looked so long and big and endless—and here it was gone! It was gone, but he'd been so busy he'd never even thought of Shadrach and his empty crib until Grandpa had mentioned it. He stood still, remembering how awful he had felt about Shadrach, and then about Rem taking Grandpa's pole and leaving him behind. And it had all turned out so fine! It amazed him. He stood stock still in the street, hands deep in his pocket, and he took a big deep breath. He puckered his lips and let out his breath hard. Out came a whistle! He'd whistled! He tried it again. Why, he could whistle!

He went dancing down the street, stopping every now and then to try out his whistle. He still could! First he'd run home to show Mother, and then around to the carpenter shop to show Dad. "Look, Dad," he'd say. And Dad would be looking at his hands for something, but then out would come his whistle! He danced down the street.

Tomorrow after school he'd even go way out to Grandfather's farm. Oh, it would be fun to go whistling all the way to Grandpa's farm to show Grandpa. And he'd put Grandpa's pole back too, the minute he saw where Rem kept it. He wouldn't even have to move the whole pile of potato crates, He could just shove it right through that opening at the bottom of the door. He hurried home, but he quietly opened the house door, quietly slipped down the hall, his puckered lips ready. He heard his mother in the kitchen. Oh boy, he could whistle—not just one short breathy blast—he could keep it going. He could whistle loud and fine!

CHAPTER 10

Shadrach was gone! He was really gone now. He'd been gone for hours. He wasn't in the hutch, he must have squeezed out between the slats again but still he wasn't anywhere in the barn. Shadrach wasn't anywhere.

Oh, it was sure now. He'd been in this awful, still barn for hours, and he'd hunted everywhere. Nobody knew he was here. Everybody was Sunday-afternoon-napping in the whole village, and it was so quiet that everything seemed to stand still. Inside of him everything stood still, like a stone. And he couldn't run to anyone, because he was supposed to be sleeping, too. He wasn't supposed to be in the barn on Sunday afternoon in his Sunday clothes.

Quiet as it was, quiet as he sat—nothing came out of the black corners of the dark barn, nothing came slowly hopping over the earthen floor. Nothing moved.

Then he could no longer stand the waiting in the hopeless quiet. Once more he started searching. He'd already searched through the whole barn twice, but this time he did it on hands and knees to be close to the floor, close to the holes and tunnels and narrow passages between boxes and bags and tools where a little rabbit could be. He poked his hand into openings and tunnels, the kind of little tunnels a little rabbit could use. At times he stretched flat on the floor and reached with his arm as far as he could under and behind things. He had to set his teeth because of the thick clinging cobwebs his poking fingers broke through. He imagined spiders running over his hand down there in the dark holes and tunnels. It gave his whole body cold shivers.

He was dirty and dusty and smeared, in his Sunday clothes. He didn't care, he couldn't care—he had to find Shadrach! He crept around a big box. There right before his face was a rat hole going under the box. Crawly shivers ran up and down his spine but he forced himself to poke his hand way down the hole—because a little rabbit could be there. His hand touched nothing, he jerked it back fast, he ran back to the hutch. He sat there, just because it was far away from the rat hole.

But he suddenly turned, looked inside the little hutch, as if by some miracle Shadrach might have come back into his hutch. The hutch was as empty as it had been for hours. He thought of praying. But Shadrach had not miraculously reappeared when he finished his tight-eyed, scared little prayer, and opened his eyes and looked in the hutch again. Oh, but he hadn't taken off his cap! And that wasn't right! He jerked it off, shut his eyes tightly and prayed again. But in the awful silence he could hear the slight rustling tiny mutter his own lips made, and it sounded so much like the slight noises Shadrach made when he came hopping over the tight earthen floor of the barn, that he forgot he was praying and opened his eyes to see if Shadrach was back. There was nothing. No little black rabbit was slowly hopping toward him. Nothing moved.

Later there were voices outside the barn, Father and Mother and Rem. They were going to Grandfather's for Sunday afternoon tea. It was that late! He'd been looking for Shadrach that long! He listened to their voices in the small hope that one of them would come into the barn, but they walked by. He couldn't go out to them, his Sunday clothes were all smeared and dirty, and he knew he would start to cry. He was supposed to be sleeping. When they got into the house, Mother would find out that he hadn't been sleeping at Grandpa's at all—then somebody would come to the barn all right. He sat there hoping it would be Grandfather, and that Rem wouldn't come with him, because he knew he would cry. And now he couldn't pray any more. He put his cap back on.

Nobody came to look for him. He still sat by the hutch, waiting for someone to come. He sat listening for that, and for tiny sounds inside the barn, he kept turning his head, kept peering into the dim, dark corners of the barn—every black cluttered nook.

Then his heart stood still. He leaned forward without making a sound, his eyes stabbing into a corner where there was a post. Behind that post, almost hidden by the post, sat something black! Something black, and he hadn't seen it there before! A black little hump, that was all it looked like—just blacker than the blackness of the floor. He glanced desperately toward the door, wishing now he'd left it open a bit for a little light. But he'd closed it, so Shadrach couldn't possibly get out of the barn. Now he didn't dare to go to the door; he didn't dare move. He stared at the little black hump again. His heart was hammering against his throat as he waited for some slight movement, but the round black hump that had no real shape in the darkness didn't move at all. It didn't move, and it didn't stir from behind the post, but still it must be Shadrach. It *must* be Shadrach! Maybe Shadrach was playing a hiding game with him.

Slowly, noiselessly he slid off his box. He crept toward the post. It seemed to take forever, it was so slow, but his heart raced as if he were running hard up the dike. As he crept forward he made his plan. He kept the post between him and the silent little rabbit. He'd grab Shadrach some-how, some way—even if it was by the ears! He'd swoop his hand around that post and grab and hold!

He was so intent on his plan as he crept for-ward, there was no relief in him that Shadrach was back. First catch him—first catch him! Now only the post was between him and Shadrach.

He had it planned, now it had to go that way —quick! For the brief breath of a moment he leaned hard against the post, his hand shot around it, pounced, grabbed. He grabbed Shadrach by the skin of his neck, pulled him off the ground, held the little rabbit, scared and twisting, at arm's length as he pulled himself up from the ground by the post.

A queer, sharp squeal shrilled through the barn! That wasn't right! Something was terribly wrong! The squealing, twisting, squirming thing kept twisting in his hand, kept squealing—oh, horribly! His scared grip tightened and tightened on the skin between his fingers, and still he held the thing far away from him at arm's length, knowing something was terribly wrong. Knowing it wasn't Shadrach! It couldn't be. He went cold all over because he knew that in his hand he held a *rat*!

He couldn't let go! He couldn't—his fingers wouldn't loosen, would only tighten and tighten. Somehow he got to the door. Somehow he managed to struggle the heavy door open without getting the rat near to him. The light from the bright yard fell into the barn. In his hand he held a big black rat!

A *rat*—and in some queer way he'd known it all the time, the moment he'd grabbed it. There the rat hung, and the teeth showed, and its sharp, narrow head and its long bare ratty tail. It hung straight down. It wasn't twisting any more.

He wanted to yell for them in the house—to yell and yell. He couldn't make a sound. Then there was nothing to do but walk slowly, carefully across the yard and hold the rat far out ahead of him. His eyes kept staring at it. The house door wasn't latched, he could back into it, push it open with his back, and keep his scared eyes on the rat. He walked softly then, slowly, because it was dark in the hall after the bright yard. His throat wanted to scream again, but now the rat started twisting. Slowly he went down the long dim hall toward the busy talking voices in the bright room.

Nobody noticed him coming through the door. They were all busy talking, they were all leaning across the table, peering through the window at something on the dike. Nobody noticed him. Then his throat made a queer noise, and Rem turned. And he said to Rem, "I caught a rat."

Rem yelled: "Look! He's got a live rat!"

They all whipped around and for a brief moment everybody sat horribly staring still, and he said to them all in his tight, frog-croak voice: "I caught a rat."

Mother screamed, and Grandfather came up out of his chair. In some way—because *he* could only stand there—Grandpa grabbed the rat, then finger by finger Grandpa pulled his cramped fingers away, because they wouldn't come away by themselves—they just couldn't. Then he stood there without the rat. Grandpa had hurried away, but *he* still stood there. And then Mother grabbed him and took him in her lap and hugged him. She hugged him all dirty as he was! He cried a little. Grandmother was making soft little clucking noises, and Father had hurried out to help Grandpa. But Rem sat looking at him, and Rem said: "He goes and catches a rat with his bare hands, but now he's crying!"

"Keep still, Rem," Mother said. And Grandmother said: "Keep still, Rem." But even though Mother held him tight, he sat up straight in her lap and he was fierce at Rem. "I'm not crying about that!" he told Rem. "I'm crying because Shadrach is gone!"

It all came back! Shadrach was gone! Lost! Never to come back now! He couldn't look hard at Rem any more. He pushed his face against his mother and cried, because Shadrach was gone. And he didn't care that Rem was there!

Mother said fiercely: "Rem, can't you go out and help the men!" And Rem hurried out of the house to look at the rat.

Now he started shaking all over in Mother's

lap. Grandma was making queer little distressed noises down in her throat, and he felt queer and sick in his stomach. He fought it and sat up and told Grandma: "I wasn't scared of the rat."

"Of course, you weren't! You're the bravest little boy," Grandma said. She wanted to give him a cookie. But when she held it out he had to hide his face, the sight of the cookie made him sick. Above him he could feel Mother shaking her head to Grandma. Then they three sat so quietly, they could hear the men's voices in the yard, and Rem's.

The men's voices sounded so sure. He sat listening, hoping that Rem had told them about Shadrach, hoping that they'd go to the barn. Maybe the three of them could find Shadrach. He couldn't—maybe the three of them could.

The voices did not go away, they stayed in the yard. Then Grandfather and Father and Rem came back in the room. Nobody said anything about the rat, but he knew the rat had been taken care of. The men just didn't talk about it because Mother and Grandma hated rats; even just talking about rats gave them shudders.

He hardly cared that he sat in his mother's lap with her arms tight around him, even if Rem was sitting on the other side of the table again. But he did sit up straight, and he told Grandpa: "I caught the rat because it was so dark and I thought it was Shadrach sitting behind the post, but it was a rat. Grandpa, Shadrach got out again, and he isn't anywhere, and I've looked for hours. And then there was the rat, but Shadrach is gone."

He was glad he could tell it all to Grandpa without crying, for Rem was looking at him so, because he'd caught a rat with his bare hands.

Then Rem said: "Maybe the rat ate Shadrach! He sure was big enough."

"*Rem!*" Mother said sharply, but it was too late. In the barn he hadn't thought of the rats getting Shadrach, because he hadn't let himself think of it. But now Rem had said it, and now it was different. It took a few moments of sitting absolutely still to take the awful thought into his mind. His mind didn't move, nothing moved, everything stood still inside of him—like a stone.

"Grandpa," he said.

"Yes, Davie."

He slowly made the words. He could hear himself saying the words as he made them one after the other. It was just as if he were listening to another boy talking. He even sounded like another boy, because his voice wasn't right. "Grandpa, rats don't eat rabbits, do they?"

"No, Davie!"

Grandpa had said it as surely as if it were a sure thing from the Bible, but it wasn't so! Grandpa had said it to make him feel better, but rats could catch little slow rabbits like Shadrach! "Then where is Shadrach?" he asked Grandpa.

"He's there somewhere, Davie," Grandpa said in his slow sure voice. Grandpa was looking at him straight. "And right now your Dad and I and Rem are going to turn that whole barn upside down to find him!" As he was speaking Grandpa wasn't looking straight at him anymore, he was slowly turning toward Rem sitting next to him, slowly turning as he talked. Then Grandpa reached out and with the flat of his hand he slapped Rem hard across the face. It smacked through the room. *Get to that barn!*" Grandpa said.

Rem stumbled up and ran out to the barn.

Grandpa got up and said: "I'm sorry."

"We'll find him, Davie," Father said, and he too went out to the barn.

Later he was glad he hadn't gone to the barn

with the men, because in a little while he was sick. Limp sick—but it didn't matter so much to be sick with just Mother and Grandmother there. Grandmother put a cold wash rag to his forehead, and Mother stripped all his dirty clothes off, and she washed him. She really scrubbed the hand that had held the rat. Mother hated rats, but she'd held him in her lap right after he'd caught the rat! He let Mother and Grandma put him to bed in Grandpa's bed. "I'm not going to sleep," he explained, "because if they should find Shadrach . . ."

"We'll wake you," Mother said. But he knew she wouldn't because he had been sick. Mother and Grandma talked, but they kept their voices to a low murmur. The long steady murmur made him sleepy, and straining his ears to hear the voices of the men coming back from the barn made him sleepy.

When he awoke it was evening, but he was still in Grandfather's bed. But they were all still sitting around the table! It must be Father and Mother and Rem hadn't gone home to eat; they hadn't even gone to church! They were talking in low voices, because they thought he was sleeping. It was raining outside—he could hear it.

He wasn't sleeping. He was wide awake. He'd waked up wide awake, and from the first moment he'd known that they hadn't found Shadrach. He knew!

Grandpa was talking. "The little fellow," he said, and he sounded just as if he had said it before. "The little fellow, imagine him grabbing that sewer rat and hanging on. And not a peep out of him! Still I can't figure that rat out in the open to be grabbed—unless—yes, that's what it must be—he must have been dopey from rat poison. But just the same!"

Grandpa was proud of him! And now Dad said straight to Mother, "Your baby boy is growing up, Mother!"

Mother paid it no attention, for she said right after: "I could still start screaming for him when I think of him standing there with that dangling rat." There were little shudders in her voice, even now. He smiled to himself in the bed. He was proud that he'd caught the rat, and he thought about it, careful not to think about Shadrach. Later he'd lift his head from the pillow and ask them—but he really knew that they hadn't found Shadrach.

Rem said: "Dad!"

Nobody answered Rem.

"But, Dad!" Rem said again. Father kept on talking.

He wanted to look at Rem. It must be they were still punishing Rem for saying that about the rat eating Shadrach. He wanted to see how Rem looked with nobody wanting to listen to him. He twisted his head on the pillow to look at Rem. He got a big surprise! Dad wasn't sitting at the table with the others. Dad was standing up, drinking his cup of tea. But he had his bicycle cape on! That meant he was going out on his bicycle in the rain! But it was Sunday!

Now Dad set his cup in the saucer, making a sharp clatter. "Well," Dad was saying, "guess I'd better be on my way. It's quite a ride to Maartens' and back. It'll be sort of midnightish before I'm home again."

"But, Dad, I've been trying to tell you," Rem said. "You don't have to go way out to Maartens'!"

Now they listened to Rem. "If you'd only listened," Rem said, and now he had a crying sort of voice. It must be Rem was all but crying because nobody would listen to him. "I've been trying to tell you—I know where there's some rabbits, the other side of the village of Nes. You know! That little red house that they call 'The

Puddle' because it's standing by that pool? Well, we got way out there the other day when we were out ditch jumping, and I saw a lot of rabbit coops with all kinds of rabbits, and black ones, too. I know! I saw it across the pool because I lost my vaulting pole in there, and I was trying to get it out of the mud."

He lay marveling in the bed. The big-boy things that Rem knew, and the big-boy things that Rem did! Went way out beyond Nes and knew about a strange house that was called "The Puddle." Oh, Rem went any place, and he knew where wild duck eggs were, and where there were weasels, and storks that nested on roofs! He lay there envying Rem—then the thought struck him! Father was going in the rain way out to Maartens' to get a black rabbit! That meant that they hadn't found Shadrach, that meant that Shadrach was gone, never to come back. He couldn't let himself think about it, not yet, and he had really known about it all the time. He'd think it all out later.

Now Grandpa was saying to Father: "You can make it back and forth to 'The Puddle' in an hour or so, and come right back with a rabbit. That would be much better than to make the child wait a whole week for Maartens to buy

172

up a rabbit and bring it here on his chinaware wagon."

"Why yes, Dad!" Rem said. "We could put the rabbit in the coop, Davie'd never know, and there in the morning would be his rabbit." Rem was proud of himself now!

"Oh, you couldn't fool him," Mother said. "Davie knows every hair on Shadrach."

Among a lot of secret talk Father went out. He was going to a house called "The Puddle" for another black rabbit!

He lay in the bed thinking that he did not want the other rabbit, did not want him at all. He wanted Shadrach and only Shadrach, because Shadrach was his, and because he had to know where Shadrach was, he had to know what had happened to him, and he had to get him back.

It was hard to explain. If he sat up now and told them: "Another black rabbit would just be another rabbit, it wouldn't be Shadrach," that wouldn't explain things at all. And it would spoil the whole big surprise they had thought up for him because they were so sorry that Shadrach was gone. No, he mustn't do it!

He made his mind go instead to his dad wheeling his bicycle down a dark road through the rain to a faraway house called "The Puddle." He thought about his dad coming back with the new little rabbit. Most likely Dad would hold the rabbit under his bicycle cape to keep it snug and dry. Rem had thought of it! Rem always thought of nice things to do after he'd done something wrong. Davie didn't want the new rabbit. It wouldn't be Shadrach.

That was the last thing he thought, then sleep sneaked up on him again. He had wanted to think it all out about the new black rabbit that he didn't want, any more than he'd ever wanted two rabbits or three rabbits. Because Shadrach was his! In all the world the first living, breathing, moving thing that he had ever had—that was alive and that was his! In all the world! He had wanted to think all that, but sleep had come instead.

Now he was awake again. He was still in Grandfather's bed, but Grandpa was in bed with him. Imagine, he'd never noticed Grandpa coming to bed! Across the room in the other closet bed he could hear Grandma making soft little droning sounds in her sleep. Rem and Mother must have gone home long ago, and because he'd been sleeping, they'd just left him at Grandfather's.

He was awake, sharp wide awake. He wondered if his father was back with the new rabbit. But that wasn't the thought that had awakened him. He had come wide awake with a thought so clear, so sure, so complete, it was as if it had been said aloud to him. "But the secret room behind Grandpa's barn! But you left the secret door open. The door is open at the bottom!"

And he knew—in some way he knew—that that was where Shadrach was! He just knew! He let himself slide out of the bed. He could do it quietly because he was so wide awake. His filthy clothes were on a chair, but he had no time for clothes. He tiptoed out of the room. Outside the moon was shining cool and clear. It lit the yard. It wasn't raining any more. On bare feet he went across the cold wet yard to the barn. And everything in the moonlit night looked cold and clean and clear.

He opened the barn door full open so the moonlight could be in the barn, but he did it softly so no one in the house would hear. He wasn't scared—it wasn't really dark night! It was really evening, not night. He wasn't scared because he'd caught a rat, and he hadn't let go!

He made himself feel big and not scared because he had a big job to do in the barn. He had to move all the crates from in front of the hidden door. But first he tried it without moving the crates. He squeezed behind the stacked crates. There was the sprung door, still open at the bottom exactly the way he had left it. It must be open almost wide enough at the bottom so he could push his head through. Dad had said that if a cat could get his head through an opening he could pull his whole body through, and so could Shadrach, so maybe he could, too. He tried it. It worked, and then his head was in the dim secret room. He wasn't really scared, but that didn't surprise him. He wasn't scared because he knew that he would find Shadrach there!

He kneeled there, his head inside the secret room, but his knees and body in the barn. "Shadrach," he whispered. "Shadrach." After every whisper he listened long, and slowly his eyes got used to the inside darkness. Now he could even make out the big, tall rudder.

He heard a small noise. Small and tiny, but clear in the night stillness! It sounded like a soft, nibbling, crackling sound. Rats?

There it began again. It was coming from behind the big rudder. But he remembered to himself that he wasn't afraid of rats, and he did not need to be, he'd caught a rat! Besides, this wasn't a rat. This was Shadrach! And if it was Shadrach, he couldn't be scared, because he had to go and get him.

He had pushed his head through the door, so it must be he could pull and wriggle himself through. He tried, he squirmed and twisted, and then he was all in the room. Soundlessly he crept toward the crackling munchings. Soundlessly he peered around the rudder.

There sat Shadrach!

Shadrach was making the crackling sounds. He was nibbling and eating. Eating oats! A half-full sack was shoved behind the rudder, and in it must be oats. Rats had chewed a hole through the sack, oats rattled down through the hole, and Shadrach sat nibbling the oats as they rolled down.

Oh, he was a smart rabbit! Shadrach had gone

in here because he didn't like being starved. He'd pulled his nice green dandelions inside his hutch and sat on them, but he liked dry old, stale old oats! "Shadrach!" he whispered in admiration. Oh, he shouldn't have whispered! But Shadrach turned and looked at him, and then he came. In three short hops Shadrach came. *Shadrach!*

He leaned overwhelmed against the big rudder, the little rabbit in his arms. His rabbit! In all the world, his rabbit! Shadrach. Shadrach. Fairest, fairest, fairest. . . .

He hurried to the opening in the door with his Shadrach. Flat on his stomach, holding Shadrach between hands stretched far out ahead of him so Shadrach wouldn't get bumped, he squirmed and twisted through the opening at the bottom of the door. The part of him that was still in the big, quiet, dark room got a little cold and scared, but his head and shoulders out in the barn with Shadrach weren't scared at all. Then he was all in the barn, and then he could stand up and hold Shadrach tight against him, snuggle him again and hug him, run his lips all over Shadrach from his nose across his soft silky back. *Shadrach*.

Now if he didn't sing he would start to cry,

because he hadn't been scared in the dark, and because Shadrach was in his arms! In all the world. Oh, fairest, fairest. . . . But he couldn't sing in the barn in the night. And he wouldn't cry. He could hardly bear to let go of Shadrach when he set him in the hutch. He snatched him up again.

He dropped Shadrach back in a wild scare. Outside the barn there was a sudden scraping, jangling noise. Then he recognized it—it was Dad's bicycle! That was what it was. It was Dad just letting the bicycle fall and jangle. All the lights went on in the house. There came Grandpa in his nightshirt. There came Grandma in her nightgown. Grandma cried out to Dad in the night. "Is he in the barn? He isn't in his bed! But he isn't in that barn this time of night?"

And Father came hurriedly and stood in the wide open doorway in the moonlight, and looked at him. Father yelled back. "Yes, he's here."

He was standing at Shadrach's hutch, and his father was looking at him, and all he could do was point and point to the hutch, and look at his father. There he stood to face his father and his grandfather, and Grandma in her nightgown. He was scared now, because it was night and he had sneaked out of bed again, but this time it was in the night.

Dad said very quietly. "So you had to hunt for him once more, Son?"

He could just nod and nod his head, because he was scared and it was night, and because he was afraid that if he started to talk he would cry.

Then Dad stopped looking at him and quickly turned to Grandpa, and said: "Well, that was a fool trip for nothing to 'The Puddle' —and waking those people up! Rem knows too many things that aren't so. Those people had some hutches from years ago, and Rem must have seen some of the junk they keep in it now and he took it for rabbits—or just imagined rabbits."

Now his father looked at him again. "Don't worry, Davie, I'll go out in the morning on my bicycle to Maartens'—and I'll bring a rabbit back, we won't wait that whole week for Maartens to come!"

All he could do was to point and point, but then he could talk. "I'm glad, Dad," he said, and he could say it quietly. "I'm glad Rem was wrong, because I didn't want another rabbit. I wanted Shadrach, and Dad, LOOK!" And then he started crying.

They all came, they were looking—they looked so startled! But now he could tell Dad again: "I'm so glad, Dad, because if Rem hadn't been wrong, then I'd have two rabbits now, and I didn't want two rabbits."

Grandpa looked so startled, he looked at Shadrach in the hutch again and again. Fairest, fairest, fairest, Grandpa! But he said quietly to Grandpa: "I found him in the secret room, Grandpa. He was in there eating oats. He likes dry old oats, and he found them himself!"

Grandpa looked even more amazed. "Oh goodness, Davie, boy! It's been so long since I was a little boy and had rabbits, I'd forgotten. But cooped-up rabbits need oats, dry oats. It plumps them up from all those watery dandelions and greens. Oats, sure, boy! The little rabbit knew, didn't he? But before I forget this, too—when you feed him oats from now on, be sure to give him water. Grandma will have a little stone butter crock for you that he can't tip over in his hutch."

Grandma made a soft, fond sound, and then Grandma went right then and there to get the little butter crock—even though it was night. There she went on her bare feet.

"Sure, boy," Grandpa said softly. "But now Shadrach will be all right. Now he'll grow and be plump. Sure, boy."

Oh, Grandpa, Dad, and Grandma—fairest, fairest, fairest. He couldn't talk from happiness, but he was singing it inside. Inside through all of him, fierce, fierce, and loud and strong. Fairest, fairest, fairest, Grandpa. Fairest, fairest, fairest, Dad. Fairest of ten thousand to my soul!

He had his rabbit back again, and it was his. In all the world! In all the world, and it was his.